LOVE
TROUBLE
IS MY
BUSINESS

LOVE TROUBLE IS MY BUSINESS

Veronica Geng

1817

An Edward Burlingame Book

HARPER & ROW
PUBLISHERS, New York
CAMBRIDGE, PHILADELPHIA, SAN FRANCISCO
LONDON, MEXICO CITY, SÃO PAULO
SINGAPORE, SYDNEY

To Howard Moss

(January 22, 1922–September 16, 1987)

CONTENTS

The New Thing   *1*

Tribute   *9*

Love Trouble Is My Business   *15*

Totalled   *21*

Secret Ballot   *25*

Our Side of the Story   *31*

Macdonald   *39*

For Immediate Release   *45*

Canine Château   *53*

The Buck Starts Here   *63*

Settling an Old Score   *67*

The Twi-Night Zone   *79*

Codicil   *89*

The 1985 Beaujolais Nouveaux:
Ka-Boum!   *95*

Equal Time   *101*

Remorse   *105*

Mario Cabot's School Days   *113*

What Happened   *119*

Hands Up   *127*

More Unwelcome News   *131*

Poll   *141*

My and Ed's Peace Proposals   *147*

Pat Robertson's Catalogue Essay for a New
Exhibition of Paintings by David Salle   *151*

A Lot in Common   *157*

THE NEW THING

Inevitably it's going to be the first thought that people have, so before anybody can even bring it up, let me say that obviously it was our first reaction, too. There's no escaping it. People are going to ask—and right from the start we had to ask ourselves, even though the question is probably the last thing that should be on our minds: Are we just going to be an imitation of *Saturday Night Live*?

Of course, there are only the two of us. Right there, that should differentiate us in the eyes of the public. But as soon as Ed and I started living together, we knew we were eventually going to have to deal with this "imitators" accusation, even though there really is no way to deal with it except to honor it as a legitimate concern and then proceed from there as if the issue didn't exist. I mean, we can't get on with our life if we have to keep looking back over our shoulder all the time, wondering if *Saturday Night Live* did it first or did it better. For a while, though, we were afraid to leave the apartment or have people in for drinks, because we know that everybody has this preconception that we're trying to compete with the image they have of Laraine and Danny and Belushi and Gilda and that whole original *Saturday Night Live* group. But then we discovered that if you actually go back and look at the old *Saturday Night Live* shows, they really weren't as immoral as you remember, so right there we have a definite advantage. My relationship with Ed has an easy, natural way of offending people which, I don't know—maybe it's an outgrowth of the eighties, but it's something you didn't see on television a decade ago.

And then we plan to keep the company very small. As I said, the regulars will be just me and Ed. We've wanted to get together for years, and we think we're a good solid nucleus of talent. Ed started a bulletin board with pictures of young, new faces we considered negotiating with, but we felt that the public wouldn't go for that format. There will be an occasional guest. One of the hopefuls we've lined up is Ed's mother, who as you may know is Michael Jackson's favorite white person.

Another difference—although, don't get me wrong, we're aware that this obsession with being different is an inherent danger—is that we have many more hours to fill than *Saturday Night Live*. Which puts horrendous demands on us for material. The first few weeks, we went bananas trying to make sure we didn't repeat anything that had been on *Saturday Night Live*. Some of our early dates were just nightmares, with me sitting there staring at Ed in stark terror, afraid that if I screamed I'd sound too much like Laraine. And Ed later confessed that he was worried the whole time that he was just another Bill Murray clone. Then gradually we realized that if we eliminated everything about *Saturday Night Live*, we would have eliminated all of life itself. So we just relaxed and decided that if we can please *us*, that's achievement enough. If, on top of that, some people enjoy us, then fine.

Mainly the thing we have to resist is this constant pressure to go "farther" than *Saturday Night Live* did. O.K., so they did everything there is to do, but of course it's always possible to do it again only making it more repellent. And frankly, if you want to know the truth, it's a temptation, the way so many people look at us expecting to see gratuitous sex. We're fiercely determined not to go that route. If an idea spontaneously occurs to us and it seems dirty, then great—we're not going to censor ourselves. But once you start getting calculated about it, then you have to have even more gratuitous sex the next time to get any reaction at all. It's like what happened to the new phone company. They started out with the strategy of just openly admitting that they were going to imitate *Saturday Night Live*, with the slogan "You'll Never Know the Difference." But then one of their publicity hacks came up with a few cheap shots that certain jaded consumers said were more daring than the original, and pretty soon they were having to incorporate more and more gratuitous sex into their business practices just to keep the public scared.

So, for the most part, how Ed and I measure up vis-à-vis *Saturday Night Live* is a concern we've relegated to the back burner. If others want to keep harping on *Saturday Night Live* and how great Chevy and Gilda and Laraine and Danny—were compared to us, that's their problem, not ours. Anyway, I just don't have the emotional energy to think about it, because I'm much, much more concerned about being investigated for secretly taping all my telephone conversations with White House officials. At the moment, I'm living in constant fear that if a judge subpoenas my tapes, he's going to think they're too much like the old *Saturday Night Live*. On one of them, where I'm screaming at White House Chief of Staff James A. Baker III, I swear to God I sound exactly like Laraine. You don't necessarily set out to copy somebody, but there are only x number of ways to go with a horror scream.

Basically, my point is that in our instant electronic media culture, novelty is no longer possible. That's a lesson that has somehow eluded at least one person in the federal government—Linda Chavez, the new Reagan-appointed staff director of the Commission on Civil Rights. What a hype artist!

She's getting all this newspaper coverage for being into "reorientation" of the commission, away from good-taste concepts like affirmative action, equal pay for jobs of comparable value, bilingual education, and study of the discriminatory impact of numerical underrepresentation of minorities. This is supposed to be a "major change of course." It's supposed to be so fresh and irreverent. For her information, the identical material could easily have been done on the old *Saturday Night Live,* by Garrett Morris, whom she would probably now claim she doesn't remember. The only reason he didn't bother to actually do it was because Garrett was hip enough to know that it had already been done a million times. Plus, because even on the old *Saturday Night Live* some things were sacred.

JANUARY 1984

My friend Cathy Schine had asked me to babysit for her six-month-old son Max one Saturday afternoon, and as she went off to the Metropolitan Opera to see Beethoven's *Fidelio*, she said, "Read this"—a *New York* magazine article on *The New Show*, a TV comedy show that was coming out:

> If there's one thing certain about Lorne Michaels's new TV venture, it's that being new will be almost impossible. ". . . When we started *Saturday Night* the expectations were so low." ". . . You have to go farther the next time to get the same reaction." ". . . If we eliminated all of *Saturday Night* there'd be nothing left." ". . . Even if the show is mediocre, . . . it can only be so in the context Lorne defines."

Immediately I wanted to write something with this sound. It was a new, specialized form of a sound that always appeals to me— the sound of anxiety being rationalized. *Fine*. What a wonderfully feeble word. It's incredibly unstable—only used when it threatens to flip over into *Not fine*. Also, I had a new boyfriend, and here was an excuse to dwell on that situation: romance anxious about its newness. (It happens a lot that a found news item registers with me this way—as a hook for some personal preoccupation I wouldn't think of writing about otherwise.) *We.* I felt pleasantly optimistic using the voice of a couple, which was new for me, but "we" is another word that always seems on the verge of collapse. Its enforcement of solidarity gets to sound a little desperate. So this story was really designed to teeter on two shaky legs: "we" and "fine." *We're fine.*

At the same time, I had these words: *Laraine, Danny, Belushi, Gilda, Murray, Chevy.* They made the story easy to write; they could be repeated and rearranged and counted on for their fixed magic.

I only had two or three hours to work while Max took his nap. (I'm grateful to him for the revelation that I didn't need total militantly spontaneous privacy—that writing can accommodate the presence of other people.) By the time Cathy got home, I had a draft of half the story, read it to her, and said it was stuck—needed another element besides the new-show new-boyfriend analogy. She said, "Why don't you just go through the *Times* and find some examples of other new stuff you don't like?"

The list included "supply-side economics," but what really rang a bell was a *Times* story on Reaganesque changes at the Commission on Civil Rights. *Garrett.* I'd forgotten about the only black actor on the original *Saturday Night*—Garrett Morris —and because I'd forgotten about him, I was now determined to make him the star of the story, without falsifying his actual importance on the show.

What I most love to do is be frivolous and then swerve into blatant sincerity. I have no idea why. My hero is Preston Sturges, whose great movie comedies of the 1940s take all kinds of daring plunges from farce to sentiment. He had inexhaustible strategies for making a situation yield its opposite and switch direction. So he could allow that the world runs on greed, delusion, and injustice while he revelled in the crazy exceptions that prove the rule. Certainly I didn't have racial prejudice in mind when I started writing the story, but when the chance came to change gears this way, it was something I felt free to do because I'd seen Sturges do it.

After the story was published, I got a phone call from a woman I didn't know, Marilyn Suzanne Miller, who turned out to have written some of my favorite *Saturday Night* sketches, including the ones called *The Judi Miller Show*, where Gilda Radner played a little girl acting out fantasies in her room at breakneck speed. Marilyn and I became friends, and we both went nuts when Frank Rich, the *Times* drama critic, popped up in the *New Republic* with an attack on the show's "golden years," claiming it had betrayed the counterculture by pandering to yuppie demographics and ethnic stereotypes. He had a point—a marginal, killjoy point. I tried to write a letter of rebuttal, invoking Dan Aykroyd's Irwin Mainway, the hotshot promoter who sold dog milk to school-lunch programs. Even if the Not Ready for Prime Time Players had some faults, they gave me a better feeling than the Reagan Administration did. But that doesn't seem like critical reasoning. I'd rather just let the fantasy of this story stand as a rebuttal.

TRIBUTE

I'm not blaming the news media for this, because if their coverage of the XXIII Olympiad featured the athletes, the athletic events, and the Olympics per se, that's probably as it should be. It's right, yet in another way it's perhaps also wrong, to have overlooked certain small, unofficial things that people all over the country did to sustain the national and even international mood of Olympic pride and pain. One of these things was a thing Ed did right in our apartment. It was Sunday, August 12, 1984, about 10 P.M. New York time, during the closing ceremonies of the Olympics. Ed and I were half watching them on TV while we tried to cover our refrigerator with Con-Tact paper. It's the refrigerator Ed had for years when the apartment was his bachelor pad, and a cat he used to have had a habit of jumping on top of it and walking around and then clawing her way down the sides trying to get off, so the enamel finish had gotten all scratched and then the scratches had rusted; when I moved in a few months ago, we decided to cover the whole thing with black Con-Tact paper. Well, we were going nuts trying to cut the paper to fit around the handle and around the screws on the corners. There were scraps of Con-Tact paper all over the floor.

It must have been close to 11 P.M. New York time—at the

Olympic ceremonies they were reprising all the national anthems—when I noticed that Ed, barefoot, was walking across the kitchen with one of the scraps of Con-Tact paper stuck to the bottom of his right foot. The paper was somewhat bigger than his foot—roughly the size of a piece of typing paper—and I want to emphasize this: the backing had not been removed to expose the sticky surface. (I know this, because that's the way I apply Con-Tact paper—cutting it to shape and only removing the backing when I get a perfect fit.) It was pretty hot in the apartment—we're way up on the twenty-third floor and we had the windows open, but it was August, remember, and we don't have air conditioning—so I guess the perspiration on his foot helped it adhere to the glossy surface of the paper.

I didn't think too much about it, but I kept noticing it out of the corner of my eye, like a visual irritant, and finally—just for something to say, because it was getting a little tense in there, what with the heat and the frustration of this refrigerator project—I said jokingly, "When are you planning to take that piece of paper off your foot?"

Quietly, Ed replied, "I think I'll keep it on until the official closing of the Olympic Games, as one man's tribute to the Olympic spirit."

I let out an audible gasp. Quite simply, the man is a genius. In that improvisational, or seemingly improvisational, moment, he proceeded to unveil a technique as powerfully controlled as if he'd trained for years. Altering his gait slightly, so as to press his foot firmly on the surface of the paper with each step, for several hours he walked a fragile tightrope between tragedy and comedy. I detected no signs of cramping.

I'm aware that in some quarters "technique" is a dirty word, and I realize that Ed might come under some criticism if I harp too much on the skillfulness of his performance. Suffice it to say that it was not despite but because of his skill that he was able to celebrate so lovingly not only the greatness but, more important, the *defects* of human beings. The perfection—one might say even the imperfection—of his performance was that although it caused him to suffer minor discomfort in the last hour, it was completely pointless, aspiring neither to goal nor to glory. But is it truly pointless when, say, a scientist who could be discovering a cure for cancer discovers, instead, an infinitesimally tiny molecule with no conceivable medical or athletic implications? Isn't what really counts that the task was done just for the sheer joy of the doing? What Ed did, he did with total love and commitment. By the end of his performance, as the ABC-TV closing credits rolled down the screen and a voice on the P.A. system at the Olympic stadium intoned the concluding words "Will the choir please leave the stage," I thought less of Ed as an athlete but a great deal more of him as a person.

Surprisingly, or maybe not so surprisingly, people want to applaud the accomplishment of something they know is "difficult." But what if a man is, God help us, an original, who does something completely new and makes it look easy? In this dog-eat-dog world, I find a man like that not just an inspiration but an antidote to post-Olympic letdown. Ed's achievement by no means devalues the medals won by the official Olympic athletes in competition, but when we threw all the scraps of Con-Tact paper out the window and watched them flutter down on the ticker-tape parade, we both felt on top of the world.

AUGUST 1984

This was just an exaggeration of something that really happened. I was hanging out with the guy I based Ed on—we were in his darkroom while he printed some photographs, listening to the Olympics coverage from the TV in the living room. He was walking around with a sheet of photographic paper stuck to his foot, and said the words exactly as Ed does: "I think I'll keep it on until the official closing of the Olympic Games, as one man's tribute to the Olympic spirit." I was determined to share this with the world—and then that determination got inflated into the tributes to Ed's genius.

The tributes were heavily influenced by a New York Film Critics Awards dinner at Sardi's the previous winter. That was the year *Terms of Endearment* won a lot of awards. As people like Shirley Maclaine and Jules Feiffer were making preposterous speeches about each other's greatness, a critic from the *Village Voice,* Jim Hoberman, turned to me from another table, handed me his program as extra paper to write on, and said, "You should be taking all this down":

He made a dream reality. . . . an audible gasp in the theater . . . celebrates the defects of human beings so lovingly . . . a fragile tightrope walk between tragedy and comedy . . . that inimitable wit that belongs to this country—or the world, maybe . . . the improvisational, or seemingly improvisational, decision-evoking process on the screen—the man is a genius. . . . The man himself is an inspiration—that's a rare thing—the man is a NICE GUY—that's special. We always hear about the dog-eat-dog world. . . . Surprisingly, or maybe not so surprisingly, movie audiences do not want literacy—and what if a man is, God help us, witty. . . . a shockingly wonderful performance—his almost childlike love of risk . . . awesome breathtaking contribution.

Somebody told me my attitude toward Ed was "a mixture of love and scorn." The scorn came from Sardi's.

LOVE TROUBLE IS MY BUSINESS

Francis X. Clines, in the Sunday *Times* . . . :
"President Reagan resembled a bashful cowboy the other day when he was asked about the
apparent collapse of the 'Star Wars' talks with
the Soviet Union. . . . At his side, murmuring
something through the fixed smile that seems
required of American political spouses, Mrs.
Reagan was overheard prompting him: 'We're
doing everything we can.' . . . Out there in . . .
the President's mountainside retreat, subjects
such as the Soviet Union seem to haunt Mr.
Reagan the way vows to read Proust dog other
Americans at leisure."

This may be the only time in history
in which the words "Mr. Reagan" and "read
Proust" will appear in the same sentence.

—GEOFFREY STOKES (*in the*
Village Voice, *August 14, 1984*)

I glanced over at the dame sleeping next to me, and all of a
sudden I wanted some other dame, the way you see Mr. Reagan on TV and all of a sudden get a yen to read Proust. Not
that she wasn't attractive, with rumpled blond curls and a
complexion so transparent you could read Proust through
it—that is, as long as her cute habit of claiming a tax deduc-
tion for salon facials didn't turn up in some I.R.S. stool pi-
geon's memo to Mr. Reagan. It was taking her a little more
time to wake up than it would take Mr. Reagan's horse to

read Proust. After I'd showered and shaved and put on an old pair of pants that wouldn't lead anybody to believe my tailor was unduly influenced by having read Proust, I went back over to the bed, where I wasn't exactly planning to say my prayers—Mr. Reagan or no Mr. Reagan.

"Mr. . . . Reagan . . . ?" she whispered, fluttering her lashes, and I trusted the dazed quizzical act about as much as if she'd told me she could read Proust without moving her lips.

So I slugged her a couple of times, and I'd have slugged her a couple of more times if something hadn't told me I'd get a colder shoulder than a cult nut insisting you could read Proust as anagrams predicting the end of the world during the Administration of Mr. Reagan.

She chuckled insanely, like Mr. Reagan looped on something you wouldn't want to drink while you read Proust. Then she touched me, with the practiced efficiency of a protocol officer steering some terribly junior diplomat through a receiving line to meet Mr. Reagan—and funny, but I got the idea she wasn't suggesting we curl up and read Proust. As her hand slid along my thigh, I noticed that she wore a ring with a diamond the size of the brain of a guy who read Proust all the time, and if I'd been Mr. Reagan I'd have been dumb enough to buy her another one to go with it. But the distance between a private eye's income and Mr. Reagan's was a gaping chasm big enough to crawl into and read Proust.

I wondered if Mr. Reagan worked this hard for his dough, as I maneuvered her into the Kama Sutra position known as "Too Busy to Read Proust."

I woke to the phone shrilling in my ear like the hot line warning Mr. Reagan that ten thousand Russian missiles hurtling over Western Europe weren't R.S.V.P.ing for a let's-get-together-once-a-week-and-read-Proust party. I let it ring, hoping the caller would decide to quit and go reread Proust, and wondering why dames always ran out on me without saying goodbye—why they didn't stick around with loyal wifely fixed smiles the way they did for hotshots like Mr. Reagan. Then I found myself getting a little weepy at a sentimental popular tune that was drifting through the venetian blinds:

> The connoisseur who's read Proust does it,
> Mr. Reagan with a boost does it,
> Let's do it, let's fall in love.

> Read Proust, where each *duc* and *comte* does it,
> Mr. Reagan with a prompt does it,
> Let's do it, let's fall in love.

> I've read Proust wished that he had done it
> Through a small aperture,
> Has Leningrad done it?
> Mr. Reagan's not sure.

> Some who read Proust say Odette did it,
> Mr. Reagan with a safety net did it,
> Let's do it, let's fall in love.

"*Cherchez la femme,*" I said to myself—a phrase I'd picked up on a case where the judge gave clemency to a homicidal maniac for having read Proust—and then I went out in the rain to a bookstore where I usually browsed for dames, and found one perusing Mr. Reagan's latest autobiography. Just for fun, I looked over her shoulder and read:

For a long time, before I met Nancy, I used to go to bed early.

AUGUST 1984

What a gift! The *Voice*'s Press Clips columnist, Geoff Stokes, had found an unusually baroque item of Reagan journalism in the *Times,* and created a work of satire by adding his own conclusion: "This may be the only time in history in which the words 'Mr. Reagan' and 'read Proust' will appear in the same sentence." I was just piggybacking on Stokes's idea by putting "Mr. Reagan" and "read Proust" into *every* sentence of something. Don't know why I instinctively started doing it in a private-eye voice. A readymade generic voice—but possibly I had a subconscious memory from Raymond Chandler's *The Big Sleep;*

flipping through it later to refresh my private-eye prose rhythms, I came across this passage:

> "I was beginning to think perhaps you worked in bed, like Marcel Proust."
> "Who's he?" I put a cigarette in my mouth and stared at her. She looked a little pale and strained, but she looked like a girl who could function under a strain.
> "A French writer, a connoisseur in degenerates. You wouldn't know him. . . . You can call me Vivian."
> "Thanks, Mrs. Regan."

Writing this technically tight kind of piece imposes certain disciplines. You want every element to fit, and sometimes the fit makes an unforeseen angle on the facts—a provisional truth you want to keep faith with. You find yourself following some unanticipated logic: like, Nancy Reagan at least is a more loving wife than the *femmes fatales* of detective fiction, and Reagan at least doesn't slug her. Of course, another logical pattern I stumbled onto was that the mere word "Reagan" was a punchline. Also, there's no point in cheating on your own rules. I had to look up the Cole Porter lyrics to see how he punctuated them—to know if Reagan and Proust had to be in every line or just every stanza. (Fortunately Porter used commas and treated the stanza as one long line.)

Stokes's premise was so ripe that even writing bad lines was fun—like making lists of improbable rhymes. ("It was too early to read Proust, so I went out and bought myself a pint of 'Mr. Reagan.' ") Later I heard that some poet teaching a class discussed this piece as a near-relative of the sestina—a verse form that keeps recycling *six* nonrhyming words, which fall at the ends of the lines in a different order each time around. Three times as much trouble.

The title (which piggybacks on Chandler) has an extra meaning for me, because it's my business to love trouble.

TOTALLED

The Kaypro Corporation said yesterday that it is
investigating the possibility that millions of dollars
in computer parts are missing from a circus tent
and big trucks where Kaypro stored them.

—*The* New York Times, *September 13, 1984*

HI-LO CORPORATION, INC.
MANUFACTURERS OF "BIG BOY" MINI-COMPONENT MICRO-COMPONENTS

Inventory Report

1. WEEK ENDING: Right before the weekend.

2. ITEM CODE *(include 3-digit processing prefix and 6-digit quality-control suffix):* The little red ones. Some of the bigger ones got mixed in with this batch, though.

3. PRODUCTION LINE EGRESS LOCATION: The big plastic bucket under the big long table.

4. DISTANCE TO STORAGE FACILITY *(in meters):* Quite a ways.

5. STORAGE FACILITY SITE *(include grid coordinates):* In a big cardboard box around back. Plus more in a whole bunch of Hefty Bags over near that great big vacant lot.

6. NO./QTY. BACK STOCK: A few.

7. NO./QTY. MANUFACTURED WEEK TO DATE: Loads of them is what I heard, but I personally didn't get to watch them drop into the bucket, because I had off most of the week to go to this big accounting seminar over in that new high-rise.

8. ADD LINES 6 AND 7: Should be one heck of a lot. Notice I said *should* be.

9. NO./QTY. SHIPPED WEEK TO DATE: I don't know that much about shipping, because that's all handled in the big room up front, but from what little I know, not that many.

10. SUBTRACT LINE 9 FROM 8: Plenty. Supposedly.

11. INVENTORY PROCEDURE (*specify allowable method A, B, or C as per Advisory IP348075-83rev.*): Friday night, when the big hand was on the six and the little hand was on the four, Shorty, Peewee, Tiny, Fats, and I headed around back to make sure the big box was relatively full. It was sealed, but Shorty happened to nudge it with his toe and thought it felt real light, so he cut it open in no time flat with this dinky pocketknife they give you after you work for Hi-Lo about forty-'leven years. What we counted compared to last week was just peanuts. We'd expected to see parts galore. So we figured a slew of them were shifted over to the Hefty Bags without anybody telling us, and we went out there fairly quick, taking the shortcut down by that little-bitty shed near the big road. There were oodles of Hefty Bags, and we had a whale of a time opening them all. It took us quite some minutes. Same story: we counted a piddling number of parts where we expected scads. Well, we had a tremendous problem and about umpteen theories, so we decided to discuss the whole deal over a mess of beers at that little place run by the skinny guy. At the plant parking lot we picked up tons of secretaries plus considerable shipping clerks, and all of them plus me, Shorty, Peewee, and Tiny, but minus Fats, who was too big, piled into Shorty's teensy-weensy minibus, and so far that's about how it adds up.

12. NO./QTY. IN STOCK: Zip, or thereabouts.

OCTOBER 1984

J ust a game with all kinds of words for size and scale—prompted by the image of tiny computer parts in "a circus tent" and "big trucks." It was occurring to me that of late my writing had gotten very babyish (especially this and the babbling Ed stories), and I thought, Oh, great, falling in love has turned me into a nitwit—and I'm liking being a nitwit. A psychotherapist I was seeing then, Peter Berg, had a more attractive explanation: he said when you feel secure and happy with someone, you're more tolerant of your infantile side. Another explanation is that I had fallen in love with Janet Malcolm's "Trouble in the Archives"; I'd been rereading this report about sophisticated psychoanalysts acting out in a blindly infantile Freudian feud:

> "We were having this talk in his office about the transference and how it affects one's perception of physical appearance, and I said to him, 'You know, I always thought of you as an immense man, and it came as a great shock to me the other day when you stood up and I realized I was practically a head taller than you.' And he said, 'What are you talking about?' And I said, 'Well, just the fact that I'm taller than you.' And he said, '*You* taller than *me*? You're out of your mind!' And I said, 'Dr. V., I *am* taller than you, I assure you.' And he said, 'Stand up,' and I stood up, and he stood up, and I towered over him, and he looked me in the eye—from a good four inches beneath me—and said, '*Now* are you convinced that I'm taller than you?' So to be polite I said, 'Yes, I see.' But I thought, This guy is out of his mind."

And I thought, This is the bottom line on the way people really behave.

I was staying up in the country, where a novelist friend had lent me his studio while he was away, so this pipsqueak piece got written on his jumbo IBM typewriter in a tiny cabin in the middle of the big sticks. When I left, I forgot to empty the wastebasket under the desk, and always wondered if he went through the wastebasket and found all my drafts. *He dumps the wastebasket contents onto the desk . . . spreads out the torn scraps of paper . . . starts piecing them together . . . A woman's consciousness—the one subject that has always eluded him in his novels—and finally it's going to be revealed in all its unguarded reality . . . in her torrid unsent love letters, maybe . . . or profound musings on some woman-type secret he could never in a million years have hoped to fathom . . . or, even better, incredibly petty stuff of the kind that they, women, really think about and would never admit to a man. . . . His pulse is racing as he fits the last fragment into place. . . . This has to be a gold mine of material. . . . It's . . . it's . . . computer-part inventory forms??? This gal is out of her mind.*

SECRET BALLOT

I know that nobody can possibly know. It would be against the law. There's no way, once that curtain closed behind me—just *no way* anybody could find out what I did in there. *Nobody will ever know.* They said so. They said so on TV. They said so over and over in the weeks before the election, not just as a generalization but showing how the generalization applied to a situation like mine. They showed a young guy and his dad—a solid-workingman kind of dad—walking along a nice street with trees, sharing their ideas about the election. The main idea they shared was that even though the whole family had always been Democrats, the son, who was voting for the first time, could go into that booth and close the curtain and nobody would ever have to know what he did in there, no matter how horrible what he did in there was. Not even his parents would ever find out.

I can't tell you how reassuring this was to me. It was something that really needed to be emphasized over and over again. Because a country like this can easily get to be like China, where the secret ballot is just a joke and you're forced to feel ashamed if you think differently from your neighbors and family. I was grateful for the reminder that in the United States of America, fortunately, my shame is a completely private matter.

So it's ridiculous for me to worry that they found out. There would be no rational basis for my fear. It would be paranoid. Whatever I did in there, and I'm not telling—even if I shot up in there (which I didn't) or voted for Hitler (and I definitely didn't do anything that bad, even though it would be nobody's business if I did), even if I spit up all over myself, or made telepathic contact with the Planet of Evil—I have nothing to worry about. Let alone if I merely did an irresponsible, selfish, stupid thing that I already regret (which I don't). When I cut my seminar at 3 P.M. to vote, Mom and Dad were still at work, so they couldn't have been anywhere near the polling place. I think Sis suspects. She could have snuck out of her gym class and followed me—but as I understand it, those booths have a special device that sets off an alarm or something if you're in there and anyone tries to peek.

Just to be on the safe side, though, I've been avoiding my folks lately. I'm in my room right now, with the door locked. A minute ago I thought I heard Sis whispering through my window, *"I'm going to tell,"* but probably it was just the wind. I've really been on edge since Election Night—probably because I haven't been getting enough Vitamin C. And my folks have been acting kind of weird. When we were all in the den not watching the election news on TV, because we didn't want to give away by some unconscious flicker of expression what we each had done in the voting booth, the phone rang. Dad said, *"That must be them now."* Then he yawned and stretched in this stagy way—there was something about it that seemed fake. Mom looked right at me and said, *"Why don't you answer it, dear?"*

For some reason a chill went through me. And suddenly it was as if I was in a nightmare—a waking nightmare, where I was sleepwalking toward the phone. When I picked up the receiver, I surreptitiously pressed the cutoff button and then pretended to talk to somebody who had a wrong number. I must have been sort of uneasy.

The next morning at breakfast, Dad was reading the *Times* and I was reading the *Wall Street Journal*. We had an unspoken agreement not to engage in any post mortems about the Reagan landslide and the Democratic gains in the Senate. Instead, we were silently sharing our respect for the sanctity of the secret ballot. But out of the blue Dad said, "Well, son, *here's something that I believe will interest you.*" I don't like being tricked. A primitive instinct took over in me, and I spilled my cappuccino all over the table on purpose. As Mom leaned across me to wipe it up, she murmured in my ear, "Dear, *I don't mean to be nosy, but . . .*" There was nothing I could do but elbow the croissants off the table. Since then, I've been staying in my room most of the time. When I lined up to vote, I was given a card with a number on it, and then when I voted they took away the card. I don't know where it is now. If Sis managed to ingratiate herself with one of the poll watchers, got hold of the card, and then—but that would be completely illegal. What I did in the booth is between me and my conscience. No—not even my conscience has the right to pry into what I did in there.

They've been making a big effort to lure me out of my room, and I'm not sure why. Looked at in a certain way, it could be interpreted as suspicious. Saturday, Dad was working on the car, and he knocked on my door and said he needed help. Well, the car being my only means of transportation in case of some totally illegal emergency, I thought I'd better check it out. I went down the driveway, where Dad was standing, well back from the car, with his hands on his hips. The hood was up, and I remember how the sun glinted on the engine as he pointed at it and said, *"Why don't you stick your head in there and take a look?"*

I wasn't born yesterday. I was back in my room in thirty

seconds. I've been in here pretty steadily since then. The one exception I made was earlier this afternoon. I'd been feeling lonely and hungry, so I stepped out into the hall. Mom, Dad, and Sis were lurking there, whispering. Dad handed me a big box wrapped in gold foil and tied with a red ribbon. Mom said, *"Go ahead—open it."*

Something told me not to. *"What's that ticking noise?"*

Of course, I felt foolish as soon as I heard myself say the words "ticking noise." I thought, Probably it's just Sis snickering.

Then Dad said to me, with a strange urgency in his voice, *"Don't be silly."*

Well, nobody had to draw me a picture. I said casually that I'd open it later, after I had something to eat. Fine, they said, they were all just about to go to the supermarket and buy the makings for my favorite casserole, because I must be famished. I said I was.

Mom said, "Good. While we're out, *you go in and light the oven."*

NOVEMBER 1984

Written very fast, the day of the Congressional elections, in anger at this Republican TV commercial, which really did have a Democratic dad giving his son permission to do whatever he wanted in the voting booth. It was instinctive to go with the son's voice—he was the one with the problem, he was the one being told *in a highly suspicious manner* not to worry—but I didn't quite know what to say, so to get up steam I started out imitating the mentally disturbed repetitions that George Trow sometimes used for weird characters like this one:

> Do you remember my preference? Do you remember the way I made them nervous? That was part of the preference. Do you remember the way I made them reluctant to wear their uniforms in public? That was part of my preference. So specific, my preference. So specific, the way the little uniforms looked under a big bulky coat. Would you know me if I wore a uniform? Would you know me if I wore a bulky coat? Would you know me if I moved a step closer?

Part of writing is going on without knowing why and then saying, Hmm, what have we here? Paranoia . . . well, wasn't that heart-to-heart father-son talk really a pitch for secrecy? In the guise of a noble dad espousing free expression, the commercial was licensing yuppies to reject their parents' idealistic politics: *Probably your own dad isn't quite this tolerant, so disagree with him in the voting booth, where nobody will know.* . . . Recently I called up Hendrik Hertzberg (a good-humored and lucid explainer of politics) and asked him to straighten me out on the secret ballot. Wasn't this commercial perverting the secret-ballot principle into something reminiscent of the secret ballot circa 1932 Germany? He said, tolerantly, Well, more people did vote for the Nazis than were running around openly in the streets as Brownshirts. But he said he thought what was really bothering me was a misplaced emphasis on the secret ballot as a prime ideal of democracy; he said the ideal isn't to hide your beliefs but to do the opposite—and then, way down the line, as a safeguard against your boss or some local gang of bullies who don't happen to like the way you're expressing yourself, we have the secret ballot, like a "firebreak," just in case.

But if I'd been so reasonable, I might not have had a story about paranoia—or a chance to use some lines of dialogue I'd been collecting for a while, lines that hang there forebodingly. Exhibit A was "Now, you go in and light the oven." Oliver Hardy says it to Stan Laurel in *Block-Heads,* where it results in a huge gas explosion and Ollie's moaning yell: "Oooooaaaaaahhhhhh!" In the back of my mind, there must also have been a recollection of Pete Smith, who made hundreds of popular live-action movie shorts from the 1930s to the 1950s, called Pete Smith Specialties (*Bus Pests, Cat College, Acro-Batty, Ain't It Aggravatin', I Love Children, But!*). He often played a home handyman—putting a TV antenna on the roof, etc.; and the narration, in his own voice, was laconically ominous: *Uh-ohhhh, somebody left a roller skate at the foot of the ladder.* . . .

OUR SIDE
OF THE STORY

Anecdotal material has its place—neither Ed nor I is in a position to deny that. In fact, we got pretty deeply into that issue on our first date, drinking Rolling Rock beer at the Superba and telling all the stories we'd each heard about how horrible the other person was—stories that would curl your hair—and then finding out that while they weren't untrue, exactly, they hadn't been put into a full perspective. So we're highly aware that the anecdote in reportage, while useful, needs to be interpreted very, very cautiously.

That caution is exactly what we find lacking in the way people are now jumping to conclusions about us on the basis of these "eyewitness" reports being spread around by recent visitors to our Village apartment—not only journalists but private citizens who have come down here on junkets to see how our new regime is working out. Naturally, we hoped they would drum up popular support for our internal struggle to create a better life. We even hoped they might influence policy toward us. So much for hope. Their reports always begin with the person's breast-beating explanation of how painful it is for them to be honest about what they saw—how they had been our biggest supporters at first, and how their initial gush of sympathy gradually dried up as they were forced to confront the evidence of their senses. Far be it from us to question their sincerity, but a lot of their disillusionment is of their own creation, stemming from their original need to see me and Ed in mythic terms. Right off the bat they convinced themselves that Ed and I were going to demonstrate the impossible: that two people with bad reputations— I and Ed—could get together and be transformed overnight into a model relationship.

But I don't want to get bogged down in generalizations about what's wrong with *their* relationships to make them so desperate for a myth. Let me just take some of the specific stories they've been reporting, and deal with those. This one guy, a foreign correspondent who has actually moved into our building, has been saying he often sees a queue outside our apartment door—as he puts it, "like in Eastern Europe." From what we've heard, he goes into vivid detail about long lines of depressed-looking people shifting from foot to foot, wearing shabby clothes, carrying pathetic little parcels and lunchboxes, etc. He says one time a dowdy woman in a babushka, with a heartbreakingly small chicken she was dangling by the feet, told him tearfully that she'd been waiting outside our door for over two hours.

Now, Ed and I have been victims lately of a certain amount of economic sabotage—mainly from the Manhattan Cable TV company, Con Edison, and the phone company— and more than likely what this guy saw was a few repairmen, etc., who had failed to show up at the assigned time and then, hearing a radio or something in the apartment, assumed we were home and hung around trying to get in. As for the all too colorful touch of the woman with the undersized chicken: first of all, it was a Cornish game hen, Ed's favorite food; and second of all, the woman was his mother (who would be astonished to hear the word "dowdy" applied to herself, or "babushka" to the Hermès scarf she wears to cover her curlers). She had come over to cook dinner for Ed's birthday while we went to a movie, and she accidentally locked herself out when she went into the hall (absent-mindedly holding the game hen), thinking she heard a burglar.

It's true that Ed and I have some problems in the area of consumer goods. We wouldn't dream of minimizing that. And if some of our visitors get disenchanted when they see us using paper towels for napkins because we ran out—granted, they have a valid point, and we're working on a better-organized central system of supply. But lately one of Ed's ex-girlfriends—who of course claims that she always wished us the best and feels just awful being obliged to say anything negative about us—has been blabbing it around that we're so unhappy we don't even have enough faith in our relationship to invest in the basic necessities. She made her observations on a couple of transient visits to our place while I was away on business and Ed let her come over out of the goodness of his heart—and, I might add, her idea of "basic necessities" is a decadent bourgeois fantasy. She has gotten enormous mileage out of recounting how shocked she was when she saw that we don't have a toaster. For her information, we make toast in a frying pan because we prefer it that way.

Another thing these reports always mention is the bribes. They say Ed's and my relationship is corrupted by bribery at every level. One story that comes up over and over (always in the same words, curiously enough) is that I was seen going to various Village stores, buying stuff, and getting it wrapped in pathetic little parcels, and then later that evening was seen giving the same parcels to Ed as a bribe to keep him at home. Again, the details are accurate as far as they go, but the story fails to mention that it was Ed's birthday eve, when (using money we could have spent on a toaster) we threw a huge birthday party, at which some of the guests apparently got too drunk to put what they saw into context. On top of which, when their own rowdiness provoked a noise complaint from upstairs, they went and reported the next day that Ed and I were destabilizing our neighhbors.

Then there's the stuff about low morale—how Ed and I have such a demoralizing effect on each other that neither of us has been able to make a dentist's appointment for the entire year we've been together. The woman who's the source of this news may not have realized, as she flipped through our appointment books while Ed was in the bathroom, that we have our own priorities and are not in the habit of going to the dentist right around the time of Ed's birthday, or on other days when we have a lot on our minds—for example, when my birthday is coming up.

Oh, well—whatever we do or don't do is grist for their mill now that this revisionist line about us has set in. If Ed pinches me on the bottom in public, it's seen as evidence that we have a degenerate, sexist relationship—which makes us hypocrites into the bargain, since that's the kind of relationship we set out not to have. It doesn't occur to people that if Ed pinches me on the bottom, maybe he's doing it for exactly that reason—that he's being *ironic*.

I could go through every one of these stories—the one about us being seen drunk on the street (it was Ed's birthday, for heaven's sake!), the one about me being seen at midnight wearing dark glasses and looking "alienated" (I'd simply had too much to drink), etc. I could go bing bing bing, right down the list, but what good would it do? People just aren't skilled at interpreting what they see, and we can't spend the rest of our lives correcting them. If some intelligent, attractive person wants to move in with us for a few months and really observe us with an open mind, great. Otherwise, everybody who's interested can find out all they need to know by going to the Superba, where we still hang out, and looking at the front table, where recently Ed carved our initials in a heart. The heart was already there, along with a mess of other old carvings, and when Ed put our initials inside it, they looked raw and pale by comparison. He wanted to age them by rubbing them with cigarette ash, but I said no, I liked it that they looked fresh. I said all the other initials had probably been carved by people who hate each other now and are no longer even on speaking terms. Ed said I was right—that we were still new, even though the heart was old and ready-made.

OCTOBER 1984

In the fall of 1983, Mortimer Zuckerman (real-estate magnate and owner of the *Atlantic*) had published an Op-Ed piece in the *Times* about his views on U.S. involvement in El Salvador and Nicaragua, after a trip he'd made there with a Congressional delegation. I'd clipped the piece and put it in a raggedy manila folder with tons of other clippings. (These yield about a two-percent return, but you never know—someday you can be leafing through the folder and an ancient item in there will magically hook up with whatever is on your mind. Many promising items never make it out: 1987, "Barbara Walters: Does She Push Too Hard?"; 1985, "Rumor has it that Godard enjoys watching women play basketball"; 1984, "If I understand correctly, you're asking about how do I envision probably the getting together of the two Koreas," Reagan press conference; 1981, "Diana Trilling, Pathfinder in Morality.") Anyway, I'd saved Zuckerman's piece because of his proclaimed change of heart: "My instinct was that this was only an internal struggle, not an East-West competition, and that once again we were backing the wrong side for the wrong reason. But I returned home . . . impressed with the effectiveness of United States policy." This was on the basis of one trip where he "was told" various things by various officials.

About a year later, reading the *New Republic*, I came across an article by Robert Leiken (expert on Central America, ex-Maoist who became influential in swinging moderates to support the Contras), just back from the most recent of six trips to Nicaragua, drained of his "initial reservoir of sympathy for the Sandinistas." For all I know, Leiken's observations and conclusions were totally accurate (I used them in arguments to provoke leftists still in love with the revolution). But his catalogue of disparities between the "myths and the unpleasant truth" was so familiar it seemed generic. Sure, genres form around the truth of repeated experience, something happening the same way time after time; in this case the genre was Tales of Betrayed Revolution—nothing surprising there. But I was as uneasy with its pointillistic details as with Zuckerman's tracing of the State Department line. For someone who bowed to no man in his early sympathy for the Sandinistas, Leiken gave a lot of weight to queues and bribes, to sexist party officials in sunglasses eating lemon meringue pie while an old woman couldn't get a doctor's appointment.

But it was the form of this material, rather than any political conviction on my part, that attracted me. It could all be loaded onto the Ed couple to shape a story about the waning of romance. Probably my own romance had moved from the early "mythic" phase into the defensive phase where you don't want to hear your friends saying it looks like it's not working out. There's a sense in which the story was a naïve political experiment: if I dealt with the contradictions of this material in romantic terms, maybe by analogy I'd find out what my politics were. My boyfriend actually did carve our initials in a precarved heart (back booth, Corner Bistro) and offer to age them with cigarette ash. I loved putting that in: a way of returning the gift. It also gave me an optimistic ending that I guess you could read as vaguely Marxist. But I was just following the dictates of my genre.

MACDONALD

On page 233 of the Da Capo Press edition of *Parodies*, edited by Dwight Macdonald, there is a spine-chilling description of an oyster, that most creative of mollusks, being swallowed alive and absorbed by the digestive juices of a human being—to no other end than a rarefied, super-civilized *frisson*. The theme of *Parodies* is most brutally stated here. The devouring of one creature by another. The sea—microcosm of a cruel universe in which culture is only murder going under some other name. None of which should come as any surprise to fans of Dwight Macdonald, who lived on intimate terms with such facts through the adventures of his fictional alter ego, the Florida detective Travis McGee. Although neighbors of the author's houseboat at Longboat Key, Florida, often mistook him for a Yale-educated political essayist or literary critic or something of that sort, this book—originally published in 1960 (before *A Purple Place for Dying*) and at last back in print—is evidence of firsthand acquaintance with the creatures who populate the shores and estuaries of his beloved Florida: the devourers and the devoured.

ALEXANDER POPE—whose taste for fresh-caught pompano concealed a penchant for something a little more expensive—murder. . . .

T. S. ELIOT—the motel clerk who never dreamed that each time he set pen to paper, he was signing his own death warrant. . . .

STELLA GIBBONS—the girl whose striped bikini hid something explosive enough to turn a deep-sea charter party into a lethal and dangerous nightmare. . . .

S. J. PERELMAN—to all appearances the simple salt-air philosopher—until Travis McGee began to suspect that nobody was quite that simple. . . .

LEWIS CARROLL—the fanatic developer with a hundred ingenious scams, he drained a marshland and exposed his own deadly secret—a secret he would pay any price to hide. . . .

WILLIAM WORDSWORTH—the copper-haired corpse who seemed to float up on the beach after every hurricane. . . .

MAX BEERBOHM—"The Gator"—Never before had Travis McGee been frightened, but never before had he been pitted against a mind as monstrously formidable as his own. . . .

JANE AUSTEN—bright, petite, blonde, suntanned—she couldn't get a license to open her health spa, but she didn't *need* a license to kill. . . .

H. L. MENCKEN—the condo salesman who plied the deep waters of greed—and before he was through reeling in the biggest catch of his life, somebody or something would have a bullet in the head. . . .

RING LARDNER—just more human flotsam from the Colombia drug-smuggling underground? Or an elusive and fiendish killer? . . .

RAYMOND QUENEAU—the cynical freighter-captain who discovered it took more than charm to commit a multiple murder that spanned an ocean. . . .

CYRIL CONNOLLY—whose bait box harbored a poisonous cargo. . . .

ROBERT BROWNING—the beach-bum Apollo with the beautiful fiancée and every reason to live—until along came murder. . . .

JAMES GOULD COZZENS—Death by smudge pot in your own orange grove wasn't a pretty way to go, and only the buried past knew the ugly secret of why he died. Only Travis McGee knew why he *deserved* to die—*twice.* . . .

ROBERT BENCHLEY—the Vietnam vet who drifted freely between the glittering cabanas of the Fun Coast and the oil-stained walkways of a derelict marina—until one of his haunts became the deadly killing ground for a lethal—and purposeful—murder spree. . . .

GEORGE GORDON, LORD BYRON—Which was the impostor? He thought he knew—until he watched the sun set over the Bahamas and saw it come up on his own corpse. . . .

GEOFFREY CHAUCER—the one who started it, and now the only one who could stop it—if only somebody could prove he was still alive. . . .

NOVEMBER 1984

An editor at Da Capo Press, Rick Woodward, had asked me to write an introduction to a new edition of Dwight Macdonald's *Parodies: An Anthology from Chaucer to Beerbohm—And After*. I said O.K., because the book is beloved and there was a certain honor in being part of its return to print. But my deadline was near, and I didn't know what to write; Macdonald had pretty much said it all on the subject of parody in his preface and appendix. Then one night I was sitting around with some friends and mentioned my problem, and Donald Fagen said, "Why don't you pretend you think he's *John D*. MacDonald?" It was such an arbitrary idea (well, maybe not all that arbitrary to someone named Donald), but it called up my affection for John D. Mac-Donald's Travis McGee novels, set on the Florida Gulf coast, where I'd read them. My brother and I had just sold our father's house there; I missed Florida and wanted to write about it.

There was a passage about an oyster in my favorite piece in *Parodies*, Cyril Connolly's takeoff on an Aldous Huxley novel:

> "How would *you* like, Mr. Encolpius, to be torn from your bed, em-barrelled, prised open with a knife, seasoned with a few drips of vitriol, shall we say, and sprayed with a tabasco as strong as mustard-gas to give you flavour; then to be swallowed alive and handed over to a giant's digestive juices?"
>
> "I shouldn't like it at all!" said Mr. Encolpius, "just as I shouldn't, for that matter, like living at the bottom of the sea and changing my sex every three years. . . ."
>
> "S-s-s-s-s-s-s-s-s-s-s-s-s-s-s-s-s-s-s-s-s-s-s-suppose," said Reggie Ringworm, who stammered, etc., "vat ve thilly oythter is weally weady and villing to be ab-s-s-s-s-orbed, I mean ab-th-th-th-th-th-thorbed, by our fwiend, vat vat is in f-f-f-fact exactly ve end for which it has been cweated. Vat th-then?"

This made a connection—seafood—between Macdonald and MacDonald. It also suggested the notion of parodists as predators.

I wanted to describe the various literary figures in the style of Travis McGee jacket-blurb teasers but didn't have any around to study as examples, so just used Rex Stout's Nero Wolfe books instead. (*Murder by the Book:* "Could a book be responsible for murder? Impossible. And yet those who made the mistake of knowing its contents were goners. . . .")

Critic David Denby, who took a scholarly interest in Dwight Macdonald, told me it was "cowardly" to write this piece instead of an essay. It was. But I was inhibited by years of derision toward other humor-anthology introductions. "With tongue planted firmly in cheek"—Ian (Sandy) Frazier always claims he read an introduction beginning that way. My friendship with Sandy is based on the profound mutual pleasure of scaring each other with quotes like that. He wasn't around the office anymore—he'd moved to Montana—and I called him in panic to read him what I'd written to see if he thought it was dumb. He was in his office, a huge snowstorm had started, he had to get home fast because he had no snow tires—but he very sweetly let me read him this tantalizing suncoast stuff about orange groves and pompano. He said he liked the way it sounded as if it had been "written off of a Florida placemat."

After turning it in, I got a startled letter from the Da Capo editor: "My first job in publishing was writing jacket copy at Lippincott, and my first assignment was John D. MacDonald's *The Empty Copper Sea.*"

Later, I learned that there's a word for processes in which a system incorporates an element of randomness. "Stochastic." Heard about it from Donald.

FOR IMMEDIATE RELEASE

A Soviet journalist who received political asylum in Britain last year and turned up in Moscow on Tuesday had signed a contract to write a book on the Soviet press, a New York publisher said yesterday. . . . The Russian . . . was paid an advance through his American literary agent.

—*The* New York Times, *September 20, 1984*

Let's not beat around the bush. Ivan Hopov, whose case has been so well publicized through the organ of the *New York Times,* is one against whom I bear a grudge. As his translator, by name V. Vronsky, and being only human, I was adversely affected by his decision to default on his book contract and return to the U.S.S.R. posthaste. For example, I had stood hired by the publisher for $3,000 payment in full, upon acceptance by the publisher of the full Hopov manuscript in an acceptable English-language rendering—an endeavor of which, due to the unfortunate turn of events, I was rendered incapable. On Hopov's part, after six months he had attained no more than the original draft outline and sample chapter. Nor did he withstand the temptation of a fanciful caprice to flee from the West without explaining to me his baffling conduct. As for myself, I was let off with merely a small chit for coffee and out-of-pocket expenses.

Nevertheless, I have since received the following letter from Hopov, written in his own English. Though Hopov himself, upon arriving in the West, resembled a hapless baby when it came right down to the crunch of speaking or writing his newfound tongue, he precociously achieved an amazing fluence. So much so that my services may in any case have been rendered spurious. (Though in my esteem his English, as written, lacks the utmost literary filigree, which I would have striven to encapture, to the best of my ability, subject to the reader's judgment.) Besides all that, he became rapidly Westernized to a T. For example, he had everything. What did he have? A Betamax, a Gold Card, etc.? He did not. He had something much greater. He had the means to grasp those things and everything else worth the candle. He had a book contract. And yet, with this pinnacle of American largesse bestowed upon his brow, mysteriously he fled. Why?

But I do not want to get ahead of his own story. Let me add solely that I here disseminate his letter without recompense or fee, not because of a loyalty to Hopov, which would be surely ill placed, but on a point of principle. If we in the West—including such an habituated émigrée as myself, so to say—could delve deep into the curious turn of the Soviet mind as it sets foot in a democratic society, it would really blow the roof off and there would be much light shed. In Hopov's bizarre renunciation (in fidelity produced below) we see the complex case of an individual, smacking of a totalitarian bent, who found himself face to face with freedom of expression and could not come to terms.

—V. VRONSKY

My dear Vronsky,

I've been hearing things—that I behaved in an unprofessional manner, that I'm a prima donna, that I left you and a lot of other people in the lurch. Well, I can't help it if people feel that way. All I can say is, I was naïve—but boy, did I grow up fast. I'm sorry if you came out of it badly, but that's your problem. If I know those bastards, they bought you off with a few bucks for expenses. What a ripoff outfit! The last straw for me was when my so-called editor wrote this really stupid jacket copy and then went into a copy-proud snit when I wanted to change it. Get this: "A sassy look at the Soviet press." "Sassy"??!! Talk about witless—and what was I supposed to do, let that go through and then look like an idiot? I know, I know—the book-buying public understands that the author didn't write the jacket copy, the jacket copy isn't even meant for them, it's meant for the reviewers who just regurgitate the jacket copy instead of bothering to write reviews, it's *supposed* to be stupid so they don't have to type any unfamiliar thoughts when they're copying it under their own bylines. I know all that. But the idea of having something like "sassy" on your very first book just poisons the whole experience. I wasn't digging in my heels—I might have been able to live with it if she'd changed it to "savvy"—but she wouldn't even listen to me. She had a tape of a ringing phone that she'd play whenever I mentioned the jacket copy, and she'd say she had to take another call and would get back to me. Which was a lie. She was really getting off on the power of making me wait for her calls. Maybe not consciously—but it was so manipulative. I don't see how this makes me a prima donna. Try telling any farmer or coal miner that his work is going to be described nationwide as "sassy" and that he won't even be allowed to discuss alternative wording. He'd be on the next plane to Moscow, just like me.

But let me start at the beginning. First of all, the contract was a joke. I think my first agent, Morty, an underling at the Stepin Fetchit Agency, must have been in a conspiracy with the publisher. But what did I know? At that point, my English was so bad he could have showed me a paper that said "Screw you and the boat you came in on" and I'd have signed. When he called me in London, he threw around a lot of names—Svetlana, etc. A snow job. (None of which checked out later, by the way.) Then he sent me a People Express plane ticket. So I went to New York and signed. There I am, churning out my little sample chapter during the day and studying English at night by working my way through *Publishers Weekly* with a dictionary. Needless to say, my curiosity got the better of me and I translated my own contract. Instant shock-horror. The reserve-for-returns clause was so watertight the book could have been a best-seller and I wouldn't have seen a nickel in royalties until the year 2050 or doomsday, whichever came later; there was no guaranteed budget for promotion; and I had no jacket-copy approval.

Then the publishing house turns out to be the pits. When I hand in the sample chapter and outline, I get a note from the publisher—just one word scrawled in the center of a piece of stationery: "Marvelous!" Is that pretentious, or what? When I'm assigned to my editor, Little Miss Tin Ear (who bad-mouthed *you* from Day One, in case you don't know), it turns out they have a good-cop, bad-cop routine going there. The "Marvelous!" notes pile up in my mailbox while she's hassling me to write with more "sass." *This is all very interesting, Ivan, but we publish junk.*

Finally, after weeks of trying to get through to Mort, who's stopped taking my calls, I nab him outside his office. "Look," I say, "my contract is ludicrous, I haven't gotten my first payment—what's the story? *PW* has pictures of my publisher lunching with movie stars at Le Cygne and meanwhile I'm licking the wastebasket."

"Ivan," he says, "Ivan, they're a marvelous old house. They publish Shakespeare. They publish Jack London."

"Great," I say. "So Jack London and I are licking the same wastebasket."

He was no help at all. So that was when I switched over

to Milt, the superagent. He came on very simpatico. And the deal was, he'd buy off Mort and renegotiate my contract. By this time I wasn't such a babe in the woods, and one thing I insisted on was that they commit themselves contractually to a ten-week promotional tour *up front*—twenty major cities, with me going on all the TV shows and then writing the book about what it was like to go on them. I'd compare and contrast going on Carson, Merv, etc., with the promotional situation in the U.S.S.R.

Some superagent. He told me I was being unreasonable and immature, that I expected him to make me overnight into a combination of Jerzy Kosinski, Barbara Walters, and Jack London. Which is ridiculous. He did nothing for me. Absolutely nothing. He claimed he'd finally wrung my advance out of them, and when I asked where was the check, he said it was being held in an escrow account as a reserve against returns, because I had no "track record." This was about the time all hell broke loose with the jacket copy and Tin Ear. God, do I hate her. She's on the end of my nose dancing and I can't flick her off. So in desperation I called Milt, and they wouldn't put me through—his secretary said he'd get back to me after he took his cat to the vet. A week goes by. Nothing. This, mind you, is a guy who sails into the office around noon, chats on the phone with a few call girls, and then has a three-hour lunch at Le Cygne with all the other superagents, where they talk about how their clients need too much hand holding.

That's the line on me now, from what I hear. That I needed too much hand holding. And I'll tell you something, Vronsky—they're right. I wasn't in it for the money—I still don't know where the money is or how much there is or if there is any. I was in it for the attention, and I'm not ashamed to admit it. I need to have my hand held. Not only do I crave it, not only do I require it to be able to work—I insist upon it, and I insist upon it all the time. And I'll tell you something else—over here, I get my hand held night and day. They have a special guy assigned to me whose only job is to hold my hand. Sometimes he holds both hands at once. Not only that, but while I'm typing this there's another guy here whose job is to stand behind me and massage my temples. I get all the attention I need. Over here I'm famous. I'm the writer who gave up an American book contract.

Best,

I. HOPOV

DECEMBER 1984

Tore the quote out of the paper because it was a chance to have fun doing a Russian-in-translation voice. I used to run into Joseph Brodsky at parties, and always liked the pleasure he got out of trying every possible English idiom. Though of course he did it with flair, unlike my earnest translator character. One time Brodsky offered to introduce me to Hans Magnus Enzensberger (a name he knew meant nothing to me beyond a pale connotation of intelligentsia) and then added, "This will really blow the roof off." So I put that in. Writing as "Vronsky" seemed natural because that was my nickname around then, started by a friend who was reading *Anna Karenina*.

Then just piled on every typical writer's grievance. Sandy Frazier had told me about going in to his publishers', Farrar, Straus, & Giroux, where Roger Straus came up to him in the hall, said just the one word "Marvelous!" and walked away. The divinely colorful lines about "licking the wastebasket" and "She's on the end of my nose dancing and I can't flick her off" were verbatim from a tirade against publishers by an agent. (Actually he said "licking the toilet" but I precensored it for *The New Yorker*.)

The one true thing I'm sorry I used came from Cathy Schine: she had written a novel, *Alice in Bed*, and her editor at Knopf put "sassy" in the jacket-flap copy and didn't want Cathy to change it. I forgot to ask Cathy if it was O.K. to use this; the horrible word was the perfect word—I forgot that *le mot juste* was real. Also, I was preoccupied with a personal vendetta of my own. A woman writer I'd once thought of as a romantic rival had been criticized in a magazine article as so demanding of her agent and publisher she had to have "her hand held all the time," and I was elated at surreptitiously turning her into a Soviet hack. Anyway, Cathy was horrified to see the "sassy" reference in print; she was afraid her editor would recognize it and think the whole story was a transcript of Cathy's rantings against her. This made me much more careful about asking permission, and less willing to entertain the idea that art is worth hurting anybody.

CANINE CHÂTEAU

(A DOCUMENT FROM THE PENTAGON'S ONGOING
PROBE INTO A DEFENSE CONTRACTOR'S $87.25 BILL
FOR DOG BOARDING)

Dear Secretary Weinberger:

I have received your request for particulars about the "nau-
seating" and "preposterous" bill run up at this establishment
by Tuffy. I would be more than happy to supply details—I
would be *delighted.* As someone who devotes his life to the
humane treatment of animals, I welcome this opportunity to
enlighten the Department of Defense and the Congress, neither of which seems to have the faintest idea what a dog
requires.

Before I get into that, however, may I point out that Canine Château is far from being some little fly-by-night dog
dorm with a few bunk beds, a Small Business Administration
loan, and a penchant for padding its bills to make ends meet.
We have been a major and highly profitable concern since
1981. Up until that time, I had been a tool designer at Low-
Bid Tool & Die (in Van Nuys), running a private specialty
shop called Jeff's Claw Clipper out of my office. (And I suppose I'm going to get in trouble for *that* now with the I.R.S.)
They phased out my job in favor of a computer when Low-
Bid won the contract to produce the "manicure kits" (I think

you know what I'm talking about) that President Reagan sent as gifts to Saudi Arabia. But I wanted to remain within the industry, and I realized the potential for expanding Jeff's Claw Clipper into a full-service kennel targeted specifically to the defense-contract segment of the pet-boarding market.

I had heard of a lovely old Spanish Colonial mansion for sale up on Mulholland Drive, and as soon as I saw it I knew it was absolutely right. At first I ran into all kinds of opposition—zoning boards, mortgage officers, you name it—but these people very quickly came around when they found out who our clientele would be. We are now the largest (and, to my knowledge, the only) kennel in California catering exclusively to the special needs of defense-contractor pets. These animals, as you may know, are extremely high-strung, and are vulnerable to kidnap by agents of foreign powers who might wish to extort from defense contractors certain classified information (such as details about the offensive capability of purported "tie clasps" regularly shipped by the U.S. to El Salvador). This is a particular danger during sensitive arms-negotiation talks. No kennels could be more relaxing and safe than ours: Canine Château, nestled on a sunny, grass-carpeted five-acre site behind bougainvillea-twined fencing of 33-mm. molybdenum-reinforced warhead-quality steel with FX-14 radial vidicon sensors and zinc-carbon detonators; and, farther south on Mulholland in a newly renovated Art Deco villa, Maison Meow, similarly secured. (Birds, goldfish, and so on may guest at either location, depending on space availability.) We are constantly upgrading these facilities, thanks to the many satisfied pet owners who generously donate not only their technological expertise but also a good deal of materials and equipment that would otherwise just be thrown away at the end of the defense-contracting workday and carted off to a garbage dump or landfill site (at government expense), where it would serve no conceivable purpose except to pollute the environment.

All things considered, then, perhaps I may be forgiven if I preen myself somewhat on our success and our high standards—aesthetic, hygienic, technological, *and* financial. Canine Château operates under my close personal supervision, and I have something of a reputation among the staff as a strict taskmaster. I wear the key to the pantry around my neck on a platinum chain; and not only is the level in the kibble bin measured twice a day but the bin itself is equipped with a state-of-the-art laser lock, which cannot be opened without a microcoded propylene wafer issued to select personnel only after the most rigorous security check of their backgrounds and habits. Waste of any kind is simply not tolerated—let alone fraud.

Now, as to Tuffy's bill. Tuffy's one-week stay at Canine Château was booked under our "No Frills" Plan. We are hardly a dog pound, of course, but I suspect that even you, Secretary Weinberger, with your military-barracks frame of reference, would find Tuffy's accommodations Spartan. We have had dogs in here—and I'm not going to say *whose* dogs they were, but I think you know the ones I mean—who have run up astronomical bills on shopping sprees at our accessories bar. I'm not criticizing them; most of these dogs are accustomed to a California standard of living, and we can't just suddenly alter a dog's life style, because the dog won't understand and will become morose. Nor am I suggesting that you, Secretary Weinberger, would seek favorable publicity at the expense of innocent animals whose taste for luxuries was created by profits in the very same industries that you depend upon for the perpetuation of your own livelihood and the good of the country. However, I question the Pentagon's decision to pay without a peep such previous bills as $3,000 for one golden retriever's ion-drive–propulsion duck decoy with optional remote aerial-guidance system and quartz-fiber splashdown shield, and then to quibble over Tuffy's, which was relatively modest.

But enough. As you requested, I am enclosing an annotated itemization of Tuffy's bill, which I trust will carry my point.

Very truly yours,

JEFF CHATEAU

President, Canine Château

——————— TUFFY 2/11/85–2/18/85 ———————

Catalina Suite .... @ $40 = $280

[All "No Frills" accommodations are suites, and this is our cheapest rate. If it seems a bit steep, consider that each suite is actually an individual bunker, deployed with gyroscopic mounts on an elliptical underground track and activated to a speed of 35 m.p.h. by random changes in the earth's magnetic field. This is a security precaution and, we feel, an essential one.]

Variety Menu (Mature Dog Cycle), plus tips .. $340

[I suppose that you, Secretary Weinberger, when *your* family goes away, would be just thrilled to have a neighbor shove a bowl of something through the door once a day. Well, an animal is no different. Our gracious waiters and waitresses are trained to make each animal's regular mealtimes as relaxed, enjoyable, and *safe* as possible. They carry conventional Geiger counters at all times, and constantly monitor food, water, and serving utensils with a combat-type bacterial scanner.]

Valet $15

[Dry-cleaning of hand-knitted dog sweater. This was February, remember, and winter in the Hollywood Hills can be cruel.]

3 Cases of Marinated Mouse Knuckles $156

[Obviously a computer billing error, as this item is served only at Maison Meow. We will be pleased to delete the charge from the original invoice.]

Contribution $100

[A tax-deductible voluntary charge to support our lobbying efforts in Congress for continuation of the tax-deductible status for this charge.]

Insurance $10

[Indemnifies us against layoffs, work stoppages, and rises in the wholesale-price index.]

Cost Overrun $245

SUBTOTAL: $1,146.00

Discounts

[We then applied our discount schedule, which allows us to maintain a high volume of business while welcoming guests from a wide range of economic brackets: not just executive animals but those at entry level in the defense-contracting and subcontracting industries, whose owners may be privy to compromising information about seemingly innocuous items manufactured for the U.S. government. The discounts were offered at our discretion and may be revoked at any time (for instance, if government-required paperwork increases our operating costs).]

Discount for booking 30 days in advance.... $400

Special discount for off-peak arrival and
departure $275

Reduction for booking through a state-
certified pet-kennel reservations agent .. $149.75

Quantity refund for four or more stays
per annum when the prime interest
rate is at or below 15% $200.00

Rebate for using Teamsters-approved
pet-carrier................................. $34

DISCOUNTS: $1,058.75

SUBTOTAL: $1,146.00
LESS DISCOUNTS: $1,058.75

TOTAL: $87.25

[Our billing is calculated by the same model of computer used to regulate the range finder on a Polaris submarine. We have every confidence in its conclusion that $87.25 is neither too low nor too high a price to pay for peace of mind.]

MARCH 1985

Sandy had come back from Montana for a few days, and we got together to show each other work in progress the way we used to do in the office. He had a half-written piece where a pool party of characters out of a bad short story suddenly gets strafed by "Krauts!" I had a couple of paragraphs based on this news item about the Pentagon paying dog-boarding expenses, and he immediately starting spewing lines: "No-frills plan . . . Do you have any *idea* what a dog requires? . . . Incredibly Spartan—he had to share a secretary with fifteen other dogs. . . . We have had dogs in here—and I'm not going to say *whose* dogs they were . . ." We decided a long time ago that the help we give each other evens out, but sometimes I have to stop him so I won't feel too reliant on his jokes. On the other hand, the line "I would be more than happy . . . I would be *delighted*" hardly sounds like writing at all, and it might seem absurd to credit it, but I worship Stanley Kubrick's ear for trite dialogue and took the line from *The Killing*. A mature couple who wish to remain anonymous supplied the title, "Canine Château"—a term they use for being in the doghouse during domestic spats.

The *New Yorker* rejected the first version of this; they just said, "No one laughed once." It didn't have the military-hardware stuff in it, and was written in more of a gay-guy dog-groomer voice. I sent it to Michael Kinsley, editor of the *New Republic*, and he called me up and said, "Why are you making fun of gay hairdressers when your real target is Pentagon over-spending?" He was so right, so precise, that I wanted to redo it for him, but I'd already been revising it to avoid the gay voice and felt I had to show it to the *New Yorker* again, and they bought it. I'd put in a lot of insane weaponry-and-explosives writing that they'd liked in an earlier piece. I lift terminology out of a 1917 infantry manual and a book called *The Way Things Work* and mix it all up. Maybe because my father worked for the Army all his life, I love the sound of "33-mm. molybdenum-reinforced warhead-quality steel."

Seeing me hell-bent on fixing and selling this piece, my boyfriend said he'd never known I was "like a gila monster." This has nothing to do with anything, but right around then it was nice that I got to participate in his work in a memorable way, which I wrote up in my diary:

Sunday, March 17, 1985
We went up to 121st St. in Harlem to photograph Clarence Norris (Willie, he's called), the last living "Scottsboro Boy."* He lives in a

---

* In Scottsboro, Alabama, in 1931, nine black teenagers were falsely convicted of raping two white women. The U.S. Supreme Court twice overturned the convictions, but a series of retrials and new convictions kept five of them in jail till the mid-1940s. In 1966 an Alabama judge released supressed evidence that conclusively proved the innocence of all nine. Clarence Norris had gone North after his parole in 1946, and was granted a full pardon in 1976.

big red-brick apartment building with good security. A woman lives with him, & she let us in. We had been told [by the photo editor] that "he's 93 and senile." So when a big strong 50-year-old man appeared, I thought it was the son and waited for him to bring out the old man. Instead, this was the old man. He was actually 72. He had on a shiny dark-blue cotton jacket, and the woman kept kvetching about how he should change into something nicer, or button the jacket.

He was kind of stolid and quiet at first, but after a while the woman asked us what we thought of the Goetz case & he opened up & told us about how people will "kill you for a dime" as he knew well from all those years in jail. He kept emphasizing that if you lock someone up and "scorn and revile" them for something they didn't do, it is guaranteed to turn them into a killer. All the while, there was a smell of corned beef and cabbage and an apple pie cooking for Sunday dinner.

Later on he changed, at the woman's insistence, into a pin-striped jacket. She showed us the book he wrote after he got pardoned by Gov. Wallace. He began to go on obsessively about injustice, and I realized that my first impression—that he was impatient with people coming around doing publicity on him for something that happened 50 years ago—was completely wrong; that he will probably be obsessed with it till the day he dies, and wanted to tell us all about it. When we shook hands to leave, he said to us, "I'm very proud to have met you," which is what we should have said.

THE BUCK
STARTS HERE

"Our attitude is, it is up to Kohl."

—*A White House official, on the Bitburg invitation (in the* New York Times, *April 26, 1985)*

Dear President Mitterrand:

Would you mind dealing with this batch of invitations that President Reagan has received? We are enclosing all the unanswered invitations to date, plus a Xerox copy of his calendar, a supply of accept/regret note paper bearing the Presidential seal, and a rubber stamp of his signature. We rely completely on your Gallic elegance in handling any potentially embarrassing requests in a graceful way. For instance, this card asking the President to appear on June 16th to serve coffee and doughnuts to demonstrators outside the South African Embassy as a symbolic gesture of support for their acts of conscience in protesting apartheid—well, obviously the President would be concerned about feelings of annoyance that he might cause Prime Minister Botha to suffer. Possibly that one could be forwarded to Botha himself to deal with. Also, there's that group of Contra unwed mothers who want the President to go down there for a baby shower. That's touchy—perhaps you could ask Mrs. Thatcher to fill in. But you will know best, given your national tradition of social graces—Proust, *"Répondez, s'il vous plaît,"* etc. The important thing is that President Reagan be spared any troublesome incidents that might arise if he made these decisions himself. That is why we hope you will graciously consent to act in his stead.

Thanking you in advance,
INVITATION WATCHDOG UNIT
The White House

Dear President Marcos:

We are writing to ask if you have the time to go over the enclosed draft of the 1986 State of the Union Message and just pencil in any changes and additions you think would be advisable. Normally, the President of the United States does this himself, but we are worried that opinions or facts in the speech might be attributed to President Reagan and create an unfortunate situation here. He has authorized us to assure you that not a word of your copy will be edited without your consent. Naturally, should you wish to come to the Capitol to deliver this address yourself on national television, your round-trip fare would be complimentary.

Best,
GAFFE PREVENTION TASK FORCE,
Presidential Speechwriting Staff

Dear President Gorbachev:

Perhaps you will find this request to be an unusual one, but please read on before dismissing it out of hand. Could you possibly substitute for President Reagan at a summit meeting between President Reagan and yourself? This would mean, of course, that you would be wearing "two hats," so to speak. But the advantages for both sides would be considerable. The President himself could not make concessions to

the Soviet Union without losing face. You, however, in sub-
stituting for him, would be in a position to be more flexible,
and no subsequent opprobrium would attach to the President's person. Any agreement that resulted would be signed
by you and by you. At a time when national leadership must
double its efforts for the good of all mankind, we hope you
will rise to this great vacuum.

Very truly yours,
SURROGATE SELECTION COMMITTEE
U.S. Department of State

APRIL 1985

Written very fast during a period of cabin fever alone in a rented house out on Long Island, near the beach. It was pretty bleak and rainy, and there wasn't much to do except read the newspapers and find fault with what the people in the newspapers were saying.

Bitburg was one of those symbolic events that everybody wants to weigh in on. This piece is probably the equivalent of "pack journalism." It must have been written automatically; my only memory is that by the time I got to the third letter, to Gorbachev, some kind of rabbit had to be pulled out of a hat, and I fell back on a tautological style of joke I'd learned from Alexander Zinoviev's encyclopedic satire of Soviet society, *The Yawning Heights:*

> The Ibanuchka River was dammed. It overflowed, flooded a potato field (the former pride of the Ibanskians) and swelled into a lake (the present pride of the Ibanskians). And for this all the inhabitants, with one or two exceptions, were decorated. The Leader made a long speech about it in which he analysed everything and outlined everything. . . . The speech was prepared by Claimant with a large group of helpers. This fact was kept somewhat secret, in the sense that everyone knew about it except the Leader, who was decorated for it and then given a further decoration because he had been decorated.

ᛋETTLING
AN OLD SCORE

"There are some experiences which should not be
demanded twice from any man," [George Bernard
Shaw] remarked, "and one of them is listening to
Brahms's Requiem." And, in his most famous
dismissal of the work, he referred to it as
"patiently borne only by the corpse.". . . There are
no rights and wrongs in criticism, only opinions
more or less in conformance with the consensus of
enlightened observers over time. By that criterion
Shaw was "wrong." But . . . musical polemics
fade far faster than music itself, thankfully.

—JOHN ROCKWELL *(in the* New York Times,
July 15, 1984)

To anyone who has tried to sit down and just enjoy a compo-
sition by Johannes Brahms, the sensation is all too familiar.
As the musical phrases begin to wash away the cares of
the day, transporting one into a delightful never-never land
of artistic transcendence, one's brain is rudely skewered
by George Bernard Shaw's unforgettable dictum about
Brahms: "Like listening to paint dry." Once Shaw penned
this zinger, it became impossible (even for an independent-
minded music critic like myself) to relax and surrender to the
simple pleasure of knowing that Brahms is no longer considered passé. And another thing: each time a Brahms piece
is ruined by an ineradicable nagging memory of that effort-

less Shavian one-liner, the annoyance is nothing compared to what Brahms must feel, squirming eternally in his grave, his reputation forever etched by the acid of Shaw's scorn.

Brahms was but one victim of Shaw's many pinpricks in the hot-air balloons of his era's cultural biases. Yet a host of the myriad names he lambasted have nonetheless survived. Yet so has a lingering respect for Shaw. In the mind of today's critic, this poses a problem. Must we say that Shaw was "wrong"? We may be tempted to utter a definitive "Yes," while on the other hand bearing in mind that critical truth is an ever-shifting flux of historically relative pros and cons. Shaw's derision of all the things he had scorn for has stood the test of time—because what he said has remained a touchstone, memorized and quoted again and again by generations of critics willing to encounter such a mind at the height of its powers even though we may possibly disagree, living as we do in a differing cultural context.

By way of qualification, however, I should point out that Shaw was not merely a negative hatchet man. For example, take his blistering assertion that "Brahms makes the lowest hack jingle-writer look like Mozart." Even someone such as myself who unashamedly rather likes Brahms (when well performed) is forced to concede Shaw's positive foresight in defending the populist craft of the jingle writer. (Not that this means I must obsequiously agree with every single last nuance of Shaw's statement.)

In any case, Shaw's poison-tipped barbs were aimed at such a multitude of targets that to say he missed once or twice would be to say very little at all. Whatever the topic, Shaw never left any doubt as to where he stood:

On *Hamlet:* "A tour de fuss."

On Oscar Wilde: "A man out of touch with his funny-bone."

On the Code of Hammurabi: "The sort of thing that would be considered profound by girls named Misty."

On the formation of a local committee in Brighton to study the feasibility of allowing tourists to transport their beach gear on special storage racks affixed to the sides of buses: "A worse idea hasn't crossed this battered old desk of mine in lo, these many moons."

From 1914 to 1919, Shaw's razor-tongued gibes were overshadowed by a vogue for bright quips about World War I. By 1921, however, he was again riding high—thanks to a series of personal appearances billed as "Shaw and His Skunk of the Week." Playing to packed houses that rocked with expectant hilarity when he led off with one of his typical catchphrases—"Am I hot under the collar tonight!" or "Here's something that really steams my butt"—he administered verbal shellackings to contemporary follies and pretensions ranging from *Peter Pan* ("It has plot holes you could drive a truck through") to the scientific community's renewed interest in Isaac Newton's idea of putting a cannonball into orbit ("One of those notions worth thinking about while you clean your teeth: a tour de floss").

For the next twenty years, nothing and no one seemed safe from Shaw's merciless stabs—not even his fans. Abhorring the nuisance of uninvited visitors, he posted on his door the following notice:

RULES FOR VISITORS

1. If you don't see what you want, don't be too shy to ask. Probably we don't have it anyway.

2. If the service is not up to snuff, just holler. Nobody will pay you any mind, but your tonsils can use the exercise.

3. We will gladly cash your check if you leave your watch, fur coat, or car as collateral. No wives or in-laws accepted.

4. If you are displeased in any way by the attentions of the resident Doberman pinscher, just remember—things could be worse. You could be at a Brahms concert.

But his visitors, instead of feeling rebuffed, copied out the notice and awarded it pride of place in their dens. Thus, a truism became widely established once and for all (until recently): that the name of Johannes Brahms was a joke (even to people who had never heard a note of his music), and that George Bernard Shaw was an unimpeachable debunker of sacred cows. Indeed, by 1940 so secure was Shaw's reputation that there was only one person in the entire English-speaking world capable of cutting him down to size.

LYNDON BAINES JOHNSON was a young congressman from Texas when, in July, 1940, Shaw came through the state on a lecture tour of the U.S. At the Houston airport, Johnson headed the delegation of local celebrities assigned to greet the distinguished visitor from abroad, who was to address a luncheon at the Houston Junior League Tea Room and then spend the night as Johnson's guest at his ranch (which probably he wasn't rich enough to own yet, but it could have been a summer rental). Waiting on the tarmac, Johnson took a minute to riffle through the press release he had been given on Shaw, and remarked, "This son of a bitch has got some kind of mean mouth on him." So Johnson was really up for a confrontation. Whereas Shaw was too busy hating Brahms to be bothered thinking about a junior U.S. congressman whom he hadn't even heard of yet. As soon as they met, Johnson immediately established dominance by a tactic he later became famous for—his "laying on of hands." The spindly, white-bearded Irishman, who didn't like being mauled by strangers, tried to counterattack by snapping at the big Texan in boots and Stetson, "What is this—some kind of tour de horse?" But it came out sounding pretty feeble. Nobody laughed, and Shaw lost crucial momentum. Johnson sensed right away that he had the edge, and he kept it. He was just a master of humiliation. On the way to the Junior League Tea Room, he asked Shaw to get him his dress boots out of a gym bag that he had purposely put on Shaw's side of the seat. At that point, Shaw overthought the situation and drew a bad conclusion. He decided to just go along with everything Johnson did and cater to him, on the theory that Johnson would quit bothering him once he saw he couldn't get a rise out of him. This was a huge mistake. The more quiet and docile Shaw got, the more Johnson tortured him.

At the luncheon, Johnson pretended not to be able to hear anything Shaw said, so Shaw had to repeat himself in a louder voice and came off as strident. The whole time, Johnson sat with his body angled subtly away from him, as if they weren't really together. During the lecture, he had a phone brought to the table and called his answering service. Then there was a question period, so Johnson asked Shaw his opinion of a book, *Pratfall Into the Abyss,* which didn't exist. When Shaw said he had never heard of it, Johnson said, "What's the matter—you too dumb to recognize a joke when you hear one?," but he said it in a funny way that would have made Shaw look oversensitive if he got mad.

Then—here's another thing Johnson did. At the end of the luncheon, they were supposed to go right to the ranch, but Johnson dawdled a lot, which drove Shaw totally nuts. Finally, after a two-hundred-mile ride in a bouncing pickup truck, which Johnson drove himself—fiddling with the radio the whole time and refusing to talk, because they were alone, and if Shaw complained to anybody later he could never prove it—they got to the ranch, where the vegetarian Shaw was confronted with the sight and aroma of grotesque sides of beef barbecuing over smoking mesquite in earth trenches sodden with fat drippings. (Johnson hadn't even known that Shaw was a vegetarian—it was just a lucky break that fed into his strategy.)

The final blow was that night, when Johnson made Shaw dress up in an oversize cowboy suit with woolly chaps and showed him off like a performing monkey to a crowd of oil barons. The most galling part of it for Shaw was that by this time he had forfeited his right to protest. If he said anything now, Johnson could come back with "Well, why the hell didn't you speak up sooner?" or accuse him of being passive-aggressive. Anyway, so much of it was the kind of stuff Shaw couldn't exactly put his finger on.

Shaw's wounds were still raw the next morning when he woke up in an uncomfortable bed made out of a wagon wheel and saw hanging on a wall the following notice, framed in mesquite:

RULES FOR VISITORS

1. Never cross L.B.J.
2. Obey all rules.

Shaw later claimed that he escaped by walking a hundred and ten miles, in sandals, to a private landing strip outside Waco, where he bummed a flight to L.A. But Johnson always told reporters that while he remembered Shaw's lecture, Shaw had spent the night in Houston at a friend's who was out of town, and never set foot on the ranch. He knew this would get back to Shaw and make him feel psychologically annihilated.

In 1950, when Shaw died, his last words were "Don't tell L.B.J. I don't want to give him the satisfaction." Every year since their meeting, Johnson had bugged Shaw by sending him a Christmas card with the printed message "Thank you for your support." Johnson enjoyed this joke so much that no one had the heart to tell him when Shaw died. Every Christmas, he personally signed the card, and his secretary pretended to mail it. Although he suffered some reverses late in his own life, this annual power play lightened his spirits until the very end. He rests in peace, unlike Brahms.

MAY 1985

The music critic John Rockwell's column, "Despite Shaw's Scorn, the Brahms Requiem Endures," had appeared in the Sunday *Times* the summer before. The voice was a classic balancing act—the obsequious line on Shaw versus Sunday-supplement caution:

> Shaw . . . had a polemical position he espoused with a fierce passion—that of modernist Wagnerianism, the progressive musical current of his day. But he didn't just espouse the positive; he excoriated the negative, too, as a tireless, Anglophobic mocker of late-Victorian pomposity and pretension. . . .
>
> The [Requiem] score offended Shaw not just because he hated all requiems, being an affirmer of the life-force, but because Brahms so consciously—and, in Shaw's view, retrogressively—evoked the German contrapuntal tradition in his music. . . . As such it answered a deeply felt need of English musical audiences of the late 19th century. . . .
>
> To this Wagnerian's taste, the Requiem is an unashamedly beautiful score. . . . Of course, it takes a superior performance to purge the work's latent ponderousness.

This was a voice to crawl into. And then there was the opposite kind of popular criticism—in love with the sound of its own crabby opinions. It seemed to be a debased legacy of what

Dwight Macdonald (annotating a Max Beerbohm parody of Shaw) had described as

> Shaw's polemical style . . . the short, punchy sentences; the familiarity . . . the Anglo-Saxon vigor, the calculated irreverences . . . the peculiar combination in Shaw of arrogance and self-depreciation, of aggressiveness and mateyness, so that the audience is at once bullied and flattered; shocking ideas are asserted but as if they were a matter of course between sensible people.

As a fiction editor and as a movie critic, I'd felt surrounded by (and sometimes attracted to) responses to art that were ersatz-Shavian blends of disingenuous bafflement and testy one-liners: *Hey, maybe it's just me but this is like watching paint dry.* Years of this were distilled into a pure droplet one recent evening when I was sitting across a dinner table from a movie critic after a press screening of *Platoon* and said I thought the movie was O.K. but not as good as a Sam Fuller war movie. In full voice she sang out the single word "Wrong!" *What a pleasant, modest person Rockwell must be: "By that criterion, Shaw was 'wrong.' But . . ."*

When the *Times* piece first churned up some of these thoughts, I tried them out in a letter to Sandy, and he wrote back:

> I think "Shaw's Scorn" is a sure-fire idea. All the stuff Shaw had scorn for. And while you list that, you could just belabor the hell out of how eminent Shaw was. Did you ever see *My Astonishing Self*? It was a one-man tour de force based on Shaw's life. I went to see it out of pure hatred for the word "astonishing," which hatred was intense for a while there. That's not true—I went with my Mom, because she wanted to see it, although my hatred for "astonishing" kept me company, too. Anyway, Shaw and Shavians and the whole deal just gripes my ass.

A year later, on the energy from writing three previous pieces fast, I got to work. I'd accumulated a long list of crank dislikes and catchphrases (cat calendars, patchouli, "You and what army?" etc.), bad epigrams ("Shopping malls are the patchouli of the middle class"), and critics' formulas ("makes ——— look like ———"), and compounded some of them into a "Shaw" much broader than Beerbohm's—a feeble fourth-generation Shaw verging on Andy Rooney and assorted belligerent pundits from the newspapers in Clearwater, Florida, where my father (also belligerent) lived. (From the *Beach Bee:* "However, do allow me the opportunity to blow off my steam in a manner that will be beneficial to you and even to me.") And come to think of it, why not make Shaw take the rap for all obnoxious wit? A postcard my father had sent me in 1977 (*something told me not to throw it into that wastebasket*), from the Red Cavalier Restaurant and Bonfire Lounge in Redington Shores, Florida, was imprinted with eight house rules, the model for Shaw's Rules for Visitors:

> 1. . . . If you've sat for a respectable amount of time and have not been waited on, don't sit another minute. Wave, snap your fingers, hsst or holler. We refuse to be responsible for bad service because you have an introverted personality. . . .
> 5. . . . The management will accept your check providing you leave your dinner guest, your watch, your mink stole, your Cadillac Eldorado or Mark IV, all for collateral. We do not accept wives. . . .

Usually the last thing you realize is that you're really writing about yourself. My book of satires called *Partners* had been reviewed as an arsenal of stilletos, slings and arrows, razors, acid, lethally poised axes, etc., so I put that imagery into the descriptions of Shaw's style. But after belaboring the hell out of all this for four pages, I didn't know where to go.

Desperately, I looked around on the surface of my desk for a clue. There was a clipping of a review, by Professor William Leuchtenberg, of *Hubert Humphrey: A Biography*, by Carl Solberg:

> In vivid detail, Solberg reveals how demeaning was Humphrey's servitude to Lyndon Johnson. In 1964 the President tortured

Humphrey by keeping him in doubt to the very last second as to whether he would be his running mate, and then told him, "If you didn't know you were going to be Vice President a month ago, you're too damn dumb to have the office." . . . After Humphrey had delivered a highly effective address at the Democratic convention, Johnson abruptly ordered him to appear at the L.B.J. ranch, where he handed him a riding costume many sizes too big for him and put him on a horse that nearly threw him. [Etc.]

. . . But as [Humphrey] was dying he was told that a *Washington Post* poll of a thousand people had chosen him the greatest Senator of the past seventy-five years. "Jesus Christ," Humphrey said, "Lyndon Johnson's going to be sore as hell about this."

I've read "Settling an Old Score" to audiences a few times, and there's always a painful dearth of laughs until the surprise entrance of L.B.J. It became a pleasure to endure the silence, knowing he was waiting in the wings. You can't—or at least I can't—premeditate an effect like that. It grew out of the blind, labored failure of the story's first half. There's premeditation in passing off the two halves as an intentional whole—but that happens later, after you've discovered that your original, naïve mistake is your real material. I like having made a mistake that makes people glad to see L.B.J. again. This was the pre-Vietnam Johnson, and I'd become re-enamored of the Great Society politician, doing wrong to do right. (I hadn't yet read Robert Caro's *The Path to Power: The Years of Lyndon Johnson*. But Caro is such a great biographer that he took away my illusions without spoiling my romance.)

Sandy told me he would have given L.B.J. a *Dallas* riff: "Mr. Shaw owns six percent of Oil Field Thirteen? [*Picks up phone.*] Shut down Oil Field Thirteen!" But I took L.B.J. more personally. I based a lot of his behavior on my boyfriend (who I thought had been torturing and humiliating me by doing stuff like calling his answering machine in the middle of a conversation). The Ranch Rules for Visitors came from the time I'd gone with him to photograph the Christmas tree at Rockfeller Center and a guard told him, "Don't set up a tripod," and he said, "There are two rules here. One: No tripods. Two: Follow all rules."

What I'd discovered was my desire to redeem L.B.J. from history, as best I could, for a little while. It was upsetting to learn that some readers didn't see it that way. A woman from Virginia wrote me:

> Relative to LBJ's unspeakable character, only one aspect of which is portrayed in your . . . piece, I have wished for many years that someone would write a book:
>
> ### THE ABOMINABLE PRESIDENTS
>
> . . . TRUMAN's habitually gross language was publicly noted; but, was this impermissable trait in a President ever duly noted for its unseemliness in a White House occupant? Not that I know of. His *obscenities*.
>
> For crudeness, obscene language habitually, outrageous whoring, and, even, extremely questionable personal intimates as White House confidantes (the term the press used for Nixon's Bebe), we have had some revolting horrors. . . . For reasons I won't go into, Jerry Ford, Jimmy Carter, and now the present incumbent are appalling. . . .

A man from Florida:

> You display Johnson as the abomination he was from start to finish. I have been cognizant of all our Presidents from Taft to Reagan. My considered opinion is that Johnson has done more permanent damage to the people of the United States than any other occupant of the Oval Office in this century. If Johnson did not choose to undergo his obligations of his post as host, he should have respectfully declined. Instead, he chose the role of buffoon, characteristic of him.

This man was not alone in assuming that Johnson actually had played host to Shaw and that the piece was reportage. A right-wing political columnist named Jeffrey Hart wrote a syndicated column (headlined, in one paper, "Shaw's Texas Visit with LBJ Recalled"), in which he repeated my bogus Shavian quips as if they were authentic (adding some real ones, as if I'd overlooked the gems) and then summarized the Shaw-L.B.J. meeting as something *"The New Yorker* reported recently."

People sent me copies of this column from newspapers all

over. A man from New Haven also sent copies of his correspondence with the editor of the *Register:*

> "How do you know," you ask me, "that Geng was writing fiction and not fact?"
>
> True, one could never definitely establish the nonoccurrence of this alleged confrontation . . . without compiling a daily log for each of them. The same could be said, of course, for the celebrated tall-tale contest between Davy Crockett and George Sand on a Mississippi flatboat in 1832. But then why should it fall to your readers to prove or disprove Hart's extravagant historical claims? . . .
>
> Our culture is well enough supplied with self-congratulatory fables. . . .

Later, a reader in Indianapolis, who had asked the *Star* to print a retraction of Hart's column, sent me a copy of Hart's response:

> A friend, knowing that I was writing a book about the year 1940, forwarded the *New Yorker* piece to me. I took the piece as genuine, since it has all the marks of a genuine ancedote, including real people, real time and places.
>
> I worked it into my book. My editor thought it genuine. So did two academic colleagues, one of them an expert on Shaw's plays. A reader of the column wrote me, however, to say that the piece seemed to be a fiction and a satire. I checked a Shaw biography and found that he had not been in the United States as represented in the piece, and, as far as can be determined, was never in Texas.

Finally, I heard from a Shaw specialist at Butler University in Indianapolis, Professor Victor Amend:

> If such a meeting had ever occurred, I am certain that Shaw would have overwhelmed LBJ as he did Mark Twain.
>
> . . . When his music criticism was reprinted, Shaw appended a note in 1936 to a column that originally appeared on 12 December 1888. Shaw begins by saying, "The above hasty (not to say silly) description of Brahms' music will, I hope, be a warning to critics who know too much." He ends with the simple "I apologize."

T HE TWI-NIGHT ZONE

It is, basically, just a superstitious connection
between a chance pattern and the conditions of
the moment, not any different than putting
together black cats and bad luck.

—*The Bill James Baseball Abstract, 1985*

". . . like Stan Musial leaving St. Louis to coach
third base in an American Legion little league."

—ROD SERLING (*in* The Twilight Zone Companion)

Hey. A few years ago I had the idea that the kind of stuff I'm
interested in would make a good series of half-hour shows for
TV. But I ran up against a problem. Or, more precisely, I ran
up against what I was told by other people was a problem.

If I wanted to do a show about a guy who builds a time
machine and ends up back in Hitler's bunker, that was fine.
But if I wanted to do a show about a statistically representa-
tive sample of those people who build time machines, and
how many of them end up back in Hitler's bunker as opposed
to the 1955 Dodgers' dugout, or twenty-first-century Wrigley
Field, or any of the other varied possibilities, that was no
good.

If I wanted to do a show about a mild-mannered bird
watcher who meets the devil in human form and trades him
his soul in return for the chance to see the world's rarest bird

and then the bird turns out to be the devil in the form of Lucifer the fallen angel with wings, great. But if I wanted to do a show about a mild-mannered bird watcher who calculates the odds against his ever sighting a sea gull in Yankee Stadium, so he can devise a Trade Evaluation formula to establish *on an objective basis* whether or not it would be worth it to trade the devil his soul in return for such an experience—in that case, forget it.

Fortunately, it turned out that the number of people interested in this stuff got bigger and bigger, and as a direct result the number of people who were saying nobody was interested got smaller and smaller.

I call this the Nobody-Plays-in-Peoria-It's-Too-Crowded Effect.

So ultimately the series came into being. Maybe you remember it. If you don't, no hard feelings. Nonetheless, it is a fact that there was such a series.

It was called *The Twi-Night Zone*. And it was described as: "a hit," "powerful," "consistent," "average," "offensive," etc. What grounds are there for accepting one or more of these terms as measurably accurate? None. And when I say none, I mean there are some, but not any supported by:

1. A vast body of concrete information that has been observed, analyzed, and shown to be misleading.

2. A mutually understood methodology mutually agreed upon, which can be constantly refined until it proves misleading enough to be itself worthy of serving as the object of study.

I'd say we've got ourselves a hell of a long row to hoe here. So let's get started by generating loads of meaningfully questionable data. I have found that the synopsis form is by far the most convenient way to summarize the contents of shows. Anyway, that is the form I have used.

THE OPPONENTS

CAST

Woman......................Agnes Moorehead

There is a common but, when you stop and think about it, baffling delusion that things are true when in reality their exact opposites are true. Such is the misconception held by a woman who thinks she can sit out on her small lawn one summer afternoon without having to face an invasion of alien robots. These tiny, aggressive creatures arrive out of nowhere. (By which we mean they arrive out of somewhere that she hasn't included in her frame of reference.) They run across the grass. One of them trips and falls. Others get their feet all tangled up. She takes a pencil, pad, and calculator from her six-pack cooler and writes:

PERCENTAGE OF ERRORS ON DIFFERENT COMPONENTS OF NATURAL GRASS SURFACE

CRABGRASS	.72	ONION GRASS	.03
DANDELIONS	.07	EARTH CLODS	.03
PACHYSANDRA	.06	MISCELLANEOUS	.05
CLOVER	.04		

Or, to put it another way:

ALIEN REPULSION FACTOR (GRASS)

$$\frac{((((((C \times D) \times P) \times C) \times O) \times Ec) \times M)}{LH^*} + \left[\begin{array}{c} \text{Astroturf cost} \\ \text{per sq. ft.} \end{array} \right] = ARF \ (G)$$

(*Total Lawnboy Hours)

Confident now, she watches as the error-plagued aliens fall into disarray, then retreat and vanish. The camera pulls back and we see a sign on the house: FENWAY PARK.

Would it be more efficient to build a dome over the lawn? Yes? No? Prove it. Then drop me a card.

WAY TO GO

CAST

Dad .... Jack Nicholson
Danny .... Danny Lloyd
Janitor .... Scatman Crothers

The bond between father and son, a bond that can be severed by no one and nothing—except maybe by a grievous misinterpretation of the principles of Sabermetrics. One morning Dad finds on his office floor a Runs Created formula dropped by the janitor, who plays around on Dad's secretary's computer at night. Dad, an otherwise educated man ignorant of even the rudiments of empirical science, glues the formula inside his son Danny's Little League uniform, believing it will magically improve his lackluster performance at the plate. In the next game, Danny hits a line drive deep into the right-field corner—a triple. But when he starts to steal home on a passed ball, a drop of sweat inside his collar erases a decimal point in the formula. This alters the equation in such a way that he disappears into an alternate universe. High up in the stands, the janitor applauds. . . .

A lot of viewers took this cautionary fable as evidence of a certain apocalyptic hyperbole on my part. Sort of an "in the wrong hands" message. I have never felt that way. I will say this, however. A formula is a fragile mechanism. What it is *not* is a recipe for pecan pie. By next year, everybody who *thinks* that's what it is will find themselves shagging fly balls in the fourth dimension.

PETE'S DREAM

CAST

Pete .... Linda Hunt

Let's call him Pete. An obnoxious old-timer who wakes up one morning vaguely remembering a dream he had the night before, a dream that somehow connects the number 4192 with the fountain of youth. Obsessed by the dream's tantalizing promise, he extrapolates wildly. He plays the number 4192 in the lottery. But it's a three-digit lottery. He searches the perimeter of a circle whose radius extends 4,192 feet from his house. Nothing. He looks up the 4,192nd person in the phone book and places a nuisance call. No answer. He begins to place 4,191 more calls to the same party. Nice try, Pete. Dream on. The camera closes in on the telephone as he dials. An old-fashioned rotary dial. As the holes move in one direction, the numbers appear to go in the opposite direction. But if that were true, we would dial backward. So it is with Pete's dream. It is an illusion.

That it is an illusion, and not a fact, is not a theory or a conjecture but a fact supported by a huge bunch of other facts. Does the public accept this? Do mice wear spats? We got a zillion letters blasting this episode for being "negative." Nevertheless, it remains one of my favorites. A lot of the credit for that goes to Linda Hunt's performance as Pete, which scared the bejeezus out of me. With the audience, though, fear struck out.

OUT OF ORDER

CAST

Sportswriter .... Larry Kert

A distinguished member of that gene pool of misinformation known as the sports media. This particular specimen, late on a deadline, is leaving a coffee shop when he presses the lever on the toothpick dispenser at the cashier's desk and receives not a toothpick but an RBI. In disbelief, he tries again, and within five minutes he has 300 RBIs (one per each two-second SSC [Simulated Scoring Context]). Elated, he runs back to his office and writes an article originating the concept of Game-Irrelevant RBI.

This episode was written by Billy Martin, who was then at loose ends and submitted a few scripts. I will just throw in my two cents:

(1) Well . . . I'm a little puzzled by Billy's limited data base. Why doesn't the guy try to get additional stats from the cigarette machine, men's-room comb dispenser, etc.?

(2) Awful lot of RBIs for 0 At Bats. I'm not saying it can't be done on Walks or ESP or something, but I am saying this: We don't have enough information about coffee shops as Run Environments to evaluate whether it can be done by the average customer. If anybody wants to work on this, be my guest.

(3) This seems like a good place to bring up a concept I like better than Game-Irrelevant RBI. And that is Yogi Berra's concept, Score-Influencing RBI. Flawless.

$$\frac{\text{TOTAL RBI} \times \text{I}}{\text{I}} \times = \text{TOTAL SIRBI}$$

THE ENIGMA OF FLIGHT .500

CAST

Hypothesis	Burgess Meredith
Axiom	Franchot Tone
Corollary	Bob Cummings
Anomaly	Orson Bean

What if AAA Airlines Flight .500, peacefully en route from Albuquerque to Los Angeles, were to be swept into the parabola of a distribution curve? Not one person that I know of has ever thought to ask this. Just for fun, let's take it a step further. What if such an event, instead of showing up on conventional instruments of measurement, simply caused the *flight number* to plummet from .500 to somewhere around .000? I can't prove yet that that's what would happen, but I am satisfied that it's a realistic option, given that the problem is more or less speculative in any case.

Did I mention that this whole thing is a metaphor for the game of baseball?

HOW TO ORDER *THE TWI-NIGHT ZONE* NEWSLETTER

While I was writing this article, so many more people got interested in this stuff that answering their letters kept me from finishing it. Therefore, I've decided to continue this project in *The Twi-Night Zone Newsletter.* If you remember some of the really, really great shows we had —like the one where Count Bozeau the ventriloquist is outraged when his dummy Bozelle autonomously utters the words *pine tar*—you might want to subscribe.

If you're so inclined, please send $25 in what we commonly define as negotiable U.S. currency, plus whatever name and address your projections indicate you'll be using later this year, allowing for a two-digit margin of error. Thanks. That's for a one-year subscription—twelve issues, unless I decide it would be more logical for the United States to go over to the Norse calendar.

MAY 1985

There was a sublime item in the news: The Procter & Gamble company had been forced to change its traditional logo—a man-in-the-moon surrounded by stars—because of unstoppable public rumors that the company "tithed to Satan" and that if you held the logo up to a mirror, the curls in the man-in-the-moon's beard read "666," sign of the beast. I thought of writing a deranged memo from the guy who has to design the new logo; everything he comes up with is subjected to occult interpretations. I told this to Peter Schjeldahl, who's an art critic, and he said, "The way I'd do it would be to show the guy's de-

signs for the new logo. A swastika. An upside-down crucifix."
This had such graphic purity that it fulfilled the idea then and
there, so I never wrote it.

Then a few weeks later I got another shot at the supernatu-
ral. And when the result appeared in *GQ* magazine, people sent
in money to order the fictitious newsletter. At least they weren't
tithing to Satan. . . . Adam Gopnik, who was then the fiction
editor at *GQ*, had called me up to ask if I'd write something for a
Humor Issue. I told him I couldn't do them to order, but then
while we were chatting, he said, "What are you reading lately?"
and I looked down at the books on my bed and saw Bill James's
1985 *Baseball Abstract* and a compendium of all the old *Twilight Zone* scenarios. I told Adam, and—just as if we were in a
1950s movie about bohemian artists in Paris—he said, "Why
don't you try putting them together?"

Adam was also a Bill James fan, and was great at noticing
where I'd faltered with the voice. He knew the vocal range parody operates in. Bill James has a wonderful voice to parody—
manneristically unmannered. But even two of us working together didn't quite catch him at his most elegant, where humility and certainty are the same: "If you have nine hitters and
nine batting order slots to put them in there are 362,880 ways to
do it, and only one of them is right."

CODICIL

> Experts are now fine-combing [William Faulkner's] writings in every stage. . . . They are trying to determine . . . how—ideally—he wanted his books published.
> This posthumous literary revision—known as "authorial intention" or "final intention"—has been advanced by scholars in the last few years. . . .
> Punctuation was important to Faulkner to establish mood and thought. When he wanted to indicate introspection, he punctuated the dialogue, in his tightly compressed handwriting, with 6 to 10 dots, like this: . . . . When he wanted to show that something was happening outside the experience of his characters, he often used a long line of dashes, like this: ———.
>
> —*The* New York Times, *June 5, 1985*

Be it understood by my literary executor and his heirs and assigns that the system of punctuation explained hereunder is my posthumous intention; that it applies to each and all of my literary effects, including all and any novels, novellas, novelettes, sprawling narrative panoramas of urban horror, potboilers, and erotic classics, not excluding the "Supervising Nurse" series; and that in the case of any deviation from said system of punctuation whatsoever, howsoever printed, said deviation shall be expunged and replaced by the version that was originally intended all along in the first place.

(1) . . . . Eight dots before dialogue indicates that whatever the character says, he or she really means the exact opposite.

(2) . . . .+ More than eight dots before dialogue creates a different feeling, more like doubt or distrust. Or maybe the character is just stalling. We don't know. Instead of having the meaning be cut and dried, it's more like: Wait a minute, is this guy on the level or not? That's the realism I depict with the extra dots.

(3) //" "// Double slash marks around dialogue reveals that at the very moment this character is talking, somewhere else in the world a volcano is erupting, a war is raging, or somebody of a different race is seeing things from another perspective.

(4) (!) An exclamation point in parentheses after dialogue makes it obvious that I, the author, know that what the person just said is really stupid.

(5) *&%!*¢#??! An asterisk, ampersand, percent sign, exclamation point, another asterisk, a cent sign, a number sign, two question marks, and a final exclamation point anywhere in dialogue clues the reader in to the fact that the character has a tremendous anger against society.

(6) ——— A single long dash after dialogue adds a very downbeat note. It's just a little touch I throw in once in a while. For the mood.

(7): A colon before the beginning of a paragraph conveys a Wagnerian-overture type of effect. Power! Impact!

(8) **********A line of asterisks after a scene with kissing or sex implies another scene with vampirism or more sex.

(9) [ ] Material inside brackets suggests insanity. Maybe one of the characters feels like blowing his top. How do you show this? I want the reader to see those brackets and immediately think: Craziness! Chaos!

(10) ;;;;;;;;; A group of semicolons gives an unusual flavor. It's just a hell of an unexpected thing.

(11) *Italic print* I use all over the place. This is a bug I have. *Italic print!* I love it. It's for when a first-person or

omniscient narrator is probing psychic wounds that will never heal, which I do a lot.

(12) ——————Six dashes in the middle of nowhere (I thought of using five for this, but then I decided no, six) has the function of blasting emotion out of the uncharted waters of consciousness inside every reader, be he or she a profound philosopher or just an individual of no great brain power, because no matter who you are or what you are, you contain the mysteries of your own subterranean life, your caverns of fear, rage, desire, everything offbeat, all protected by walls of ice until suddenly, smash!—along comes the icepick of authorial intention to break it into little pieces that melt into a river of strange sensations, which no one but you is ever supposed to know about. Here is where I touch on the universal problem: that you can never, never go completely into the other guy's heart.

(13) A capital letter at the beginning of a sentence is a private joke.

I want these inserted in all my works. There's a list on my bulletin board of where they go.

FALL 1985

People thoughtfully send me clippings to use, but mostly it's because the item reminds them of something I already did—so it isn't fun for me to do again. This was the first time I used a sent-in clipping. The article "New, Authentic Edition of Faulkner Novels Set," with its examples of Faulkner's arcane punctuation philosophy, was spotted by Terry Adams, an editor at Knopf. He'd once sent me a free copy of Julian Barnes's novel *Flaubert's Parrot,* hoping I'd contribute a publicity blurb, and I'd loved the book but couldn't think what to say (Fran Lebowitz's blurb was memorable: "Flaubert's Parrot, c'est moi")—so maybe I felt under some little obligation to at least make use of his clipping.

I started writing while visiting Roy Blount and Joan Ackermann, up in the Massachusetts Berkshires. Joan had a computer, on which she was writing a book about volleyball, and taught me how to use it, but I couldn't be funny on it. The ease of manipulating bizarre punctuation combos on a computer did produce many speckled-looking pages, but it wasn't exactly writing. Then I switched to Roy's ancient manual typewriter with missing keys, but in his study there was a distracting collection of books like *The American Heritage Dictionary of Indo-European Roots*. I did get some ideas for bad sentences from an old high-school grammar text he lent me.

This piece must have taken about six different forms, over a few months. At one point, it was an Ed story. ("Quite often, writing that is not originally intended for publication is eventually found to have some literary or historical importance that makes it suitable for publication. That is why I have taken the responsibility of going through Ed's personal papers and letters with a fine-tooth comb.") Then for a while it was about this couple named The Blunts, who wrote thrillers published in miniature collectible forms—on teabag tags, bottle-cap liners, etc.—using symbolic punctuation to economize. (Joan inspired this while making a cup of tea: the staple holding the teabag tag to the string looked like a dash.)

What the piece needed was a human presence behind the punctuation mechanics. At last, trying to think of someone who explained very specifically and crudely how he got his artistic effects, I remembered an interview with Sam Fuller (in *The Director's Event: Interviews with Five American Film-Makers*):

[For *Pickup on South Street*] I told the art director I wanted those [subway] stairs, because I liked the idea of Widmark pulling Kiley down by the ankles, and the heavy's chin hits every step. Dat-dat-dat-dat-dat: it's musical.

I stole Fuller's entire voice: his vocabulary ("Impact!") and his freedom to say, Did you notice the great part where I did so-and-so? and then, Of course this other part didn't turn out as great as I wanted. His movies have dialogue like "We can't leave him behind—he'd be caught and brainwashed" (Gene Barry in *China Gate*). But that's the price you pay for his schematic method. Typical: in *Pickup,* a fat guy eating with chopsticks is offered some payoff money, and without breaking rhythm he picks up the twenty-dollar bill with the chopsticks and goes on eating. Because I love Fuller's movies, I wanted a passage of sincerity, so I put in that part about how "you can never, never go completely into the other guy's heart."

THE 1985 BEAUJOLAIS NOUVEAUX: KA-BOUM!

PARIS—According to a recent survey, 30 percent of all French people over the age of 10 never drink wine. . . . The survey found that France has lost two million wine consumers since 1979. . . . What does the decline mean for wine producers?

—FRANK J. PRIAL, *"Wine Talk" (in the* New York Times, *September 25, 1985)*

PARIS—. . . the head of the intelligence agency, Adm. Pierre Lacoste, was dismissed for having refused to disclose . . . the details of the sinking of the Rainbow Warrior.

—FRANK J. PRIAL, *"Greenpeace and the Paris Press: A Trickle of Words Turns Into a Torrent" (in the* New York Times, *September 27, 1985)*

If it's French and it comes in a bottle, how bad can it be? Such has always been the modest philosophy of this column. But with the 1985 Beaujolais Nouveaux now in, promising a strong vintage, the U.S. consumer is beginning to confront a profusion of new châteaux, varietals, arsenals, and appellations of flash point, none previously familiar here. This is all to the good for the much-needed expansion of the French export market and for Americans seeking top value for their dollar. Nonetheless, it demands that we exercise discretion and even caution. There is already a huge influx of mail to this column from uncertain readers. Today I shall deal with the most often-posed concerns.

Q —For three dollars I bought a bottle of Nuage de Fumée '85 from a man on the corner of Forty-second Street and Eighth Avenue. He assured me that if I was satisfied with it he would meet me by appointment in a Times Square hotel room with a crate full of additional selections. Is this a good idea, and can you tell me more about Nuage de Fumée? On the label it also says "Château de Gélignite," and then under that it says "13.5% nitroglycerine by vol."

A —While not, technically speaking, a Beaujolais, Nuage de Fumée is produced in the Palais de l'Élysée region near the Seine River in north-central France, on acreage adjoining (though not under the direct responsibility of) the renowned Mitterrand estate adjacent to the five-hundred-square-mile terrain closely intervening between it and the finest Beaujolais vineyards. If the label also says "Mise en bouteille au Directorat Général de Sécurité Externe," you have a first-class Nuage, partaking of the typically delightful fruitiness, thirst-quenching *fraîcheur,* and vivacious charm evoked by the Beaujolais bottle, yet boasting complex overtones of the aromatic wood pulp and potassium nitrate used as an inert base or adsorbent to balance the acidity of the nitro. The '85 is already matured and not for laying down, as it tends to go off quickly. Since your dealer is unknown to me, I strongly urge that you check his reliability by asking him to show you exactly how to wire the underwater fuses to the blasting cap.

Q —We want to send a birthday present to one of my husband's business associates in Tampa, and can spend up to twenty-five or thirty dollars. Since people have been raving about the 1985 Plastique Nouveau, I tried purchasing a case, in a magnetic gift hamper, plus an extra bottle for ourselves, from Sandy's Surplus Ordnance out here on eastern Long Island. But when we tried it, it was so disappointing. It simply blew a neat hole about the size of a quarter through our sideboard. Should I return the entire case for a refund?

A —Yes, and I congratulate you on your discernment! A true Plastique has none of the finesse you describe, and considerably more bite. It should expand with an exuberance verging on impetuousness, to bring out the full depth and roundness of the radial impact. You do not say which bottler is named on the label, but sadly there are an unscrupulous few who are taking advantage of relaxed export quotas to blend Plastique with Pomerol, Saint-Émilion, and other adulterants.

In such an unpredictable situation, one can only rely on the conscience of the retailer. I have spoken to Sandy, who confirms that he will give you a refund or credit. As it happens, to accommodate a new shipment of magnums from Corsica, he is having a sale on some classic vintages. In your price range he can custom-assemble an impressive gift pack from among the following: Domaine Algérie '58, Clos Collaboration-Nazis '41, Mouton Dreyfus '94, and La Terreur Brute 1793—all noted for their ripe bouquet and quintessentially French character. (A nice touch is that the neck of each bottle is wrapped in the sommelier's traditional pure-linen field dressing.) Or you might consider the sampler case of Château Préfecture de Police, Nuit des Barricades, the most acclaimed of the May 1968 Sorbonnes. (Includes 1 Phosphore Blanc, 1 Vapeur de Chlore, 1 Poudre Enfermée, 1 Le Gaz Orthochlorobenzalmalononitrile, and 2 Grenades Lacrymogène.)

Q —What is your opinion on my broker's advice to invest in futures of 1985 Haute Incendiaires? Any risks?

A —Naturally, all such futures carry the risk of high opening-price quotations' not holding until or before the dollar declines against a thirty-six-month delivery date, on the assumption that shortages in the '82s and '83s will incite buying of first-growths ten to fifteen percent above the previous year's *primeurs*. I suspect, however, that this is not what is troubling you. It is common and understandable for the novice American investor to feel apprehensions of a more primitive nature. An ocean away, in a foreign place called Bordeaux (not even the real Bordeaux), your precious investment is being aged in an underground facility where highly trained oenologists are employed to hand-rotate the lead casks so the bituminous sediment is uniformly distributed through the methane. Is this delicate and volatile process, you wonder, secure from terrorists? Rest assured: the French government considers this industry so vital to its national interest that it has pledged a tactical nuclear force to defend those cellars.

Now let me extend a more personal warranty. Recently, I travelled to one of the sunny French atolls for a blind tasting. The 1985 Haute Incendiaires were already showing majestically, with a "sleeper" bouquet that needs twenty to twenty-five seconds of breathing before it bursts into vigorous glow, heralding a monumentally balanced combustive structure (surprisingly high in the ratio of tannin to carbon monoxide) in which the first bright spicy flash is followed by layer after infinite layer of textural displacements so mouth-filling that there lingers on the palate the earthy flavor of the native herbs, grasses, and nearby cars and buildings, until the distinctive velvety char patterns emerge on the long, haunting, bone-dry finish.

DECEMBER 1985

A couple of years earlier, the Sherry-Lehmann liquor store, right near my apartment, accidentally printed my phone number, similar to theirs, in an advertisement. I was in Florida at the time, and whenever I called my New York answering machine for messages, it was full of wine orders. Amazing—people call a number and get a girlish voice saying, "Hi, I'm not home right now," and they just dutifully place their orders. When I complained to the store, I expected them to at least give me a complimentary bottle of champagne or something, but they did nothing. So I always wanted to get back at them.

Then, in September 1985, Marcelle Clements, who is French and reads all the American news about France to see how wrong it is, told me to check out these two *New York Times* stories written by the wine correspondent—one on wine, the other on the French press's investigations into the sinking of the Greenpeace antinuclear protest ship. Don't know if she had any inkling of how anti-French my piece would turn out to be (and I've been afraid to ask her).

I showed it to Sandy in a half-baked form; he had just moved back here from Montana, and I got reacquainted with a neutral facial expression he has when he doesn't like what he's reading. Then he said, "Put in a lot more writing about explosives." Music to my ears. What you really want to hear under those circumstances is not "It's fine" but "Look, here's something specific you're obviously interested in, so go to town with it—go wild." Concentration and liberation. . . . So in gratitude, I put his name in, as the owner of the surplus-ordnance store.

The wines were blended from descriptions in the Sherry-Lehmann catalogue and other toxic materials, including gases and grenades mentioned in *L'Insurrection Étudiante: 2–3 Mai 1968*.

EQUAL TIME

You know, recently one of our most distinguished Americans, Clare Boothe Luce, had this to say about the coming vote [on aid to the Contras]. ". . . My mind goes back to a similar moment in our history—back to the first years after Cuba had fallen to Fidel. One day during those years, I had lunch at the White House with a man I had known since he was a boy—John F. Kennedy. 'Mr. President,' I said, 'no matter how exalted or great a man may be, history will have time to give him no more than one sentence. George Washington— he founded our country. Abraham Lincoln—he freed the slaves and preserved the union.' "

—RONALD REAGAN (*address to the nation, March 16, 1986*)

WILLIAM HENRY HARRISON: He was the first occupant of the White House to eat with a knife and fork.

MILLARD FILLMORE: He had his own likeness secretly engraved in the folds of Miss Liberty's dress on the 1851 Silver Dollar.

FRANKLIN PIERCE: He earned the sobriquets Old Tongue-in-Groove and The Gabardine Gangplank.

ULYSSES S. GRANT: He translated the words to "The Star-Spangled Banner" into thirteen different languages, including mirror writing.

BENJAMIN HARRISON: He predicted the birth of the Dionne Quintuplets over forty years before it happened.

WILLIAM MCKINLEY: He was his own grandfather.

WARREN G. HARDING: He campaigned on a bicycle carved from a single giant bar of soap.

CALVIN COOLIDGE: He coined the catchphrase of the era—"Do you simply want a cigarette or do you want a Murad?"

HERBERT HOOVER: He reorganized the National Christmas Card Cemetery.

GERALD FORD: He had the idea for *Shampoo* long before the movie came out.

RONALD REAGAN: He popularized the political theories of Clare Boothe Luce.

MARCH 1986

laying Trivial Pursuit for the first time, and reminiscing about childhood board games and collections, I remembered a Presidential Coins game from the 1950s: "silver" coins stamped with the Presidents' likenesses, in a serious-looking royal-blue display box, with a set of trivia questions like "Which President's spinster niece served as his official White House hostess?" This seemed the appropriate level at which to treat Reagan's quotation of Clare Boothe Luce's inane view of Presidential history.

A tiny but amusing discipline of writing a piece like this is to get the period details right. The *New Yorker*'s fact checkers always help. The head of the checking department is a tall, scholarly-looking guy named Martin Baron. With extreme politeness, plus some sarcastic asides directed at whoever in public life happens to be perpetrating a cover-up at the moment, he will gladly explain the cause-and-effect relationships among all the minutiae that go into the determination of a fact. Martin checked this piece. He made sure Murad cigarettes were on the market in Coolidge's day (and, I'll bet, that soap existed in Harding's day). We had an interesting discussion about which of the many beautiful silver Miss Liberty coins show her dress as opposed to her face only. It was fun to work with someone who was pleased that I owned a copy of *U.S. Coins of Value*.

This book was in my possession because my brother Steve and I had inherited a random collection of coins—mostly Kennedy half dollars and Indian-head pennies—and thought of selling them while we were in Clearwater, Florida. (There's a huge number of coin dealers in that area—maybe because the senior citizens like to vary their investment strategies. You can even call a Sears Precious Metals Hotline for current prices.) One day we drove all over town looking for a dealer I'd liked the looks of in the Yellow Pages. . . . The address is a shack with the door open, next to Live Bait. . . . "This can't be it." . . . "Maybe they don't answer because too many people come looking for a coin shop." . . . "The street numbers start over again out past Ulmerton—we could drive out there. What was the address again?" . . . "Oh, Indian Rocks *Road*—that's across the bridge, runs along the other side of the inland waterway." . . . "Can you see any numbers on your side?" . . . "Eight-something. Are the numbers getting higher or lower?" . . . "There—820 . . . 816 . . . 12300? What? Maybe it's like the way the numbers start over again out past Ulmerton." . . . "We're spending more money on gas than we'll get for these stupid coins." . . . You could take a similar view of the amount of energy put into fact-checking this little piece. But I enjoyed both experiences in the same way.

REMORSE

Ed and I have an announcement to make. Before I say what it is, I would like to thank all our friends and acquaintances, as well as the many people who don't even know us but have taken such an ongoing interest in the ups and downs of our relationship merely on the basis of hearsay over the three and a half years that Ed and I have been together. Although we have often felt that their interest in us was prurient and even somewhat sinister, we also couldn't help feeling just a little bit flattered.

We could go on basking in this attention, knowing that people are awed by and, in certain cases, jealous of me and Ed as a couple. However, there comes a time when you have to consult your own conscience and do what you believe is right, no matter how disillusioning it may seem to your friends, and no matter how much it may gratify the kind of people who are always waiting to see you knocked off your pedestal.

Ed and I want to acknowledge that we have made some mistakes in the past. These were in areas which it would be pointless to go into at this late date and in the brief space we have allotted ourselves for this public statement. Suffice it to say that Ed has behaved abominably, and I have not been lily-white, either. However, we feel that it doesn't get us off the hook just to *say* we've made mistakes and are putting them behind us now. Anyone could do that, and there would be no definite way to ascertain the person's sincerity or commitment. Therefore, we have come to the following decision: The best way to affirm that we have put our mistakes behind us, once and for all, is to announce our intention to comply voluntarily with the conditions set down by the Commissioner of Baseball.

We would like to emphasize the word "voluntarily," because there is absolutely no legal basis on which compulsory compliance can be exacted from us under the terms of our contract with the New York Mets. This contract explicitly defines our agreement thus: We shall be entitled to a rain check in the event of an incomplete game, which is any game terminated before five full innings of play, or four and a half if the home team is ahead, and in return we consent to the use of our image incidental to any live or recorded video display of the game. There is also, on our part, an implied consent to confiscation of any thermos jugs we bring into the stadium. However, our attorney assures us that no court or arbitrator would interpret this as a blank check for the Commissioner to exploit at his whim. It is on the basis of choice, then, not coercion, that we have settled on our course of action, and we want this clearly understood not only by Commissioner Peter Ueberroth but by people who would like to see us forced to cringe and crawl.

As for the details of our compliance, we have mutually agreed to share these in an equitable fashion. I will be in charge of the community service. As part of that, I will be making announcements like this from time to time, thus relieving the community of the burden of prying into our personal lives for themselves or trying to find out by bothering the Mets' publicity office. I will also spend one hundred hours working with youthful offenders, who, I believe, could profit tremendously from one hundred hours away from the grind of science or math, listening instead to me explaining why I am talking to them instead of their teachers or parents. There is far too little interrelating between people like myself and youthful offenders. These are usually among the brightest and most attractive members of our society, and so—I want to reemphasize this—I consider spending one hundred hours with them *in no way a punishment* but an opportunity I gladly welcome. This, of course, is a side benefit; the main thing is that I will be giving one hundred hours during which these young people will not have a chance to engage in any offenses—at least, not if I have anything to say about it, which I very much hope I will.

Ed, being a much more intensely private person than I am, will be involved in supplying specimens for the urinalysis. Anyone who still harbors some doubt that urinalysis is one of the best ways to put your mistakes behind you simply does not understand the stringent laboratory procedures necessary to insure mutual trust. Ed will be donating ten percent of his time to provide these specimens, on a random basis. The random pattern has been worked out in consultation with the Department of Higher Mathematics at M.I.T., where a computer will convey a signal to our home-computer modem, at which time Ed will contribute the specimen and relay it to the lab via one of New York's top bonded messenger services, which will be on twenty-four-hour standby, in order to maintain the scientific integrity of the procedure.

Thanks to advances made in recent years by medical-research surveys and major corporate personnel departments, we now know that the primary cause of human mistakes is a lack of self-respect, in turn caused by an impersonal society in which no one has cared enough to monitor our body chemistries on an individual, one-to-one level in a scientific setting. Instead, we are all too often at the mercy of informal speculation by those with no special training. Ed's contribution is an effort to help change all that, and in the long run we expect it to influence sizable numbers of young people to participate in such programs themselves.

As a more direct result, I believe we are going to see a significant increase in the respect that youthful offenders will feel for Ed when I explain to them in detail exactly how much he is doing. I respect him more already myself, knowing that he will be setting an example—far more real than any textbook lesson—in the rigors of the scientific method and the richly humanistic interaction of a private individual with the society outside himself.

I will keep these remarks brief, and conclude by saying that it is with a new lightness of heart that we look forward to Opening Day. This season, as in past seasons, we fully intend to be behind first base, in the lower deck, which is where our contract entitles us to be. Our hope is that the New York Mets will accept us as worthy of being there.

MARCH 1986

T he New York Mets' first baseman Keith Hernandez was one of the players who had testified the year before at the trial of a cocaine dealer and admitted to using the drug in the past. Now the Baseball Commissioner wanted to impose retroactive penalties and drug testing, and Hernandez was saying that ought to be a matter for arbitration. The *Daily News* ran the arrogant headline "KEITH, YOU'RE WRONG!" "Wrong" meant insufficiently remorseful to gratify Shavian sportswriter Phil Pepe. (Pepe later softened his position.)

I had written an appreciation of Hernandez for *Vanity Fair* back in 1985 (just as the drug story was breaking), and a friend who read it had said, "Where's the cocaine?" It wasn't there because I hadn't seen it on the field. I was interested in the way Hernandez seems fitted to the exact scale of the game, fills it right out to the edges. For me, that was the complete story on him. This wasn't a reporter's attitude, but it was the one I had. Didn't even want to interview him—just sit in the stands or in front of the TV and take my little notes:

4/13/85 vs. Reds: 1 out, man on 2nd, Mets need a run to tie it up— KH needs to advance the runner home—fights the ball off and hits long fly to outfield—not a hit but scores a run. Another good at-bat—Mookie on, KH fights off tough pitches, draws a walk, so they can't walk Carter. . . . 4/17 vs. Pittsbgh: KH hit on arm by pitch by McWilliams. Won game with sac. RBI. . . . 5/17 vs. Giants: KH 2 spectacular plays in 1st inning for last 2 outs—a diving catch down the line, then a catch backwards over his head. . . . 5/26 vs. L.A.: KH playing 1st, waiting for the pitch, bent down, left hand always touches his glove for an instant, like a steno w/ pad and pencil poised to take down an unpredictable burst of dictation. . . . 6/21 vs. Montreal: funny out at 1st, KH about to throw to Sisk but suddenly slides face-first into base—then laughs. . . . 6/22 vs. Montreal: KH wears his uniform like street clothes. . . . 7/2 vs. Pittsbgh: McCarver, "Hernandez is not *guarding* the line, but he is *aware* of the line." . . . July: KH hit .464 in road trip where they swept Atlanta and Cincinnati.

I went along when my boyfriend photographed Keith for *Vanity Fair,* during batting practice, but I was very uncomfortable on the field. (The only other woman had a bunch of cameras around her neck—a protection against looking like you don't belong.) I'd never been so tongue-tied. I was supposed to chat with Keith, to amuse and relax him during the photo session (something I hadn't been shy to do with other subjects), but couldn't think of what to say that wouldn't sound ridiculous. Later, when I told this to another woman baseball fan, Brooke Alderson, she gave me an article called "Women, Baseball, and Words," by Adrienne E. Harris:

I get to baseball through men: fathers, lovers, husbands, buddies, students. For baseball is a social space appropriated by and for men. Women['s] . . . marginality is given and absolute. . . . To speak as a woman about baseball is to be immediately entangled with baseball's ideological function and to be at odds with it. The evidence of this confrontation is in the struggle, the rupture, the discordance between my voice and the variable but coherent male voice of base-ball.

. . . Talk, banter, commentary, analysis, evocation, taunting, the work of baseball talk is the creation and distribution of a complex male world in which real and imaginary men feel connected.

Published in a journal called *PsychCritique*, this takes a line I might normally resist. But I'd felt that inadequacy of voice while writing the article (in a faked-up tone based on rereading Roy Blount's baseball reporting), and experienced the utter impossibility of walking up to Hernandez and saying, "Hey, Keith—how 'bout those Dodgers?"

However, I'm not remotely awed by Ed. Turning Keith into Ed domesticated him and empowered me to write in a comfortable voice. It also sidestepped the risks of self-righteousness and ignorance in head-on writing about the drugs issue. I didn't even know what my opinion was until I was in the midst of writing. Making up displaced versions of real things, I can see more clearly whether I believe them.

One problem I couldn't sidestep was submitting urinalysis jokes to the *New Yorker*. The idea was to show that the drug testing was just punitive and symbolic; but initially I got carried away and had urine samples being delivered to Commissioner Ueberroth at dinner. A note about the manuscript, from William Shawn, said "No urine delivered to table." It was always tempting to try changing material Mr. Shawn found objectionable to something *even worse* but worded in a way that he couldn't possibly object to; usually that would force solutions more creative than the original crudeness. That's what happened when I took out urine delivered to table. So I'm not sorry.

Testimonial remorse is a seductive thing, with a perilous relation to the truth. Keith Hernandez later published a book, *If at First*, in which he said of his trial testimony about using cocaine, "I regret my use of the words 'massive' and 'demon.' I have no idea why I said them." That really rang true. I read it to a Mets-fan English teacher, Donald Lyons, who said, "A dazzling piece of honesty and psychological realism."

MARIO CABOT'S SCHOOL DAYS

There is no kid who's qualified to go to Harvard who can't, on some scholarship or other.

—HUGH SIDEY (*on* Agronsky & Company)

There's no reason why we shouldn't have an Italian President—we've had everything else.

—BARRY GOLDWATER (*on* 60 Minutes)

Chuck got one. It wasn't that big a deal. Chuck says all you have to do is wait for June to roll around and then go to any cash machine, insert your driver's license, and type in your S.A.T. scores in a certain sequence, and the machine issues you a four-year scholarship to Harvard. (The personal interview is a thing of the past.) Of course, your scores have to qualify, and I'm not sure what you use if you don't have a license, but apart from that it's pretty much a foregone conclusion that you'll get one—*if* you can handle the mob scene. By the middle of the summer, those cash-machine lines are a nightmare. Word has really gotten around, even though they don't announce it. It's just an open secret—like the fact that George Washington was a full-blooded Chickahominy Indian, which everybody knows, even though it never appears in print anywhere.

So I'm thinking of maybe doing that, although there's a bunch of other ways you can get one, which I'm also thinking of doing, because the way that you pick should be suited to your unique qualifications and personal interests. For instance, Gary happens to like driving, and a couple of weeks ago he was driving his van out on the Island when just past Riverhead he started to lose an incredible amount of power and the oil light went on, so he pulled into a garage that was still open, even though it was nearly midnight. There were five kids working there who, it turned out, had all gone to junior high together and now were into fixing cars instead of going to Harvard, and they got interested in Gary's problem, which was, for starters, that a few days earlier somebody had rear-ended him and now the lock on the engine compartment wouldn't open (which, if you remember, was why President Paul Robeson missed his own Inauguration and they had to swear in another guy). So this one kid, a girl in a tube top, drove her car behind his and turned on her lights so everybody could get a good view of the lock, and then they all took turns trying to jimmy it open. While this was going on, an older guy walked across the highway and came over to them—they all seemed to know him—and said he was going into the hospital at six the next morning for a bypass operation. He said, "I can't even walk from here to right over there without breaking out in a sweat." He said his doctor had told him to prepare himself for thirteen hours of surgery but he didn't know how to prepare himself, so he'd come over to see what was happening with the van. When Gary told him, he said he had exactly the same problem once when he owned a VW Beetle, so he sympathized in a big way; then he shook Gary's hand and left, and afterward Gary found pressed into his palm a token that read "Redeem at Gate for Free Scholarship to Harvard." Of course, all this depended on a certain amount of chance, but no more so than when an obscure Pennsylvania coal miner named James Polki got elected

President until the Electoral College found out a novice tele-graph operator had made a mistake—if you want to call it a "mistake" that American history includes a hardworking Polish immigrant who held the highest office in the land, temporarily.

Still, with the college term starting in September, I don't know if I can afford to wait for a lucky break. (If I had that kind of time, I could just as easily count on the rumor I read about in *TV Guide* being true—that next season they're add-ing a "Harvard Scholarship" section to the Wheel of For-tune.) So what I'll probably just do is send away for one, by printing my name and address in block letters in black or blue ink on a standard 3 × 5 file card (or a piece of white paper cut to the same dimensions) and then, below that, copying or tracing the words "HARVARD SCHOLARSHIP" from a label (it's on most of the product labels now) and mailing it in, making sure it's postmarked on or before the August 15th deadline—all of which is a little complicated procedurally, but so was the constitutional system that gave us President Thomas Noguchi (the only coroner ever to become Chief Ex-ecutive), when the individuals ahead of him in the line of succession were physically or mentally incapacitated, briefly.

So that's how I'm going to get mine. My mom and dad have accumulated enough AT&T. Opportunity Calling Credits to cash in for one, but I know they're saving them to donate to the political candidate of their choice in 1988. They feel very strongly that if contributions like that, from people with modest incomes, had been possible throughout our his-tory, President Irving Berlin would have been able to raise the fare to Washington.

Some people will tell you that none of these are legitimate Harvard scholarships, but they're the same people who will blatantly deny that in 1896 a palomino pony named Pancho, running as an anti-vivisection candidate for the Presidency, got ninety-seven percent of the popular vote. They will insist that you have to apply directly to Harvard, but that isn't true. The regular sources are all dried up by this time of year, and you have to take a more unorthodox approach—like the way a woman named Dora, or Doreen, occupied the Oval Office in 1920 as a poltergeist. She's still there (the longest term ever) and may have accomplished more than we realize—a question I plan to research when I major in Alternative American History at Harvard.

JUNE 1986

Coming back from a trip to Boston to photograph the documentary filmmaker Frederick Wiseman, my boyfriend and I bought eight live lobsters from a place called Airport Lobsters, to take as a surprise birthday present to his mother, who was staying on Long Island. On the drive out, in his 1969 Volkswagen van, we had the same experience described near the start of this piece—the garage, the kids, the guy who talked about his bypass surgery. By the time we got to East Hampton, it was three A.M., so we slept in the van. I didn't like sleeping in there with the sounds of the lobsters rustling in their ice packs, but we were afraid to put them outside, in case of predators. Then the next morning it turned out that his mother was going back to the city unexpectedly, so we had to find another venue for the lobster lunch. Linda and Aaron Asher rose to the occasion. Linda's bold handling of lobsters made us see how helpless we'd have been without her; and she had the wit to call a seafood store and ask how you tell whether passive lobsters are dead, because dead ones are toxic. We had an idyllic outdoor feast, with the radio broadcast of the Mets game wafting across the grass. (Later Linda told me she'd never been quite sure whether slow-moving live lobsters are a little bit toxic, and that sitting there in the sun, with the poppies in bloom and the glory of *enough lobster,* she'd felt "one tiny capillary of danger threading through Paradise.")

Since this experience had involved a lot of waiting around, I'd taken notes, and they seemed to hook up with the quotes I'd saved about Harvard and the Italian President, suggesting a high-school voice. (The lobsters never made it in.) Also, possibly in the back of my mind were Wiseman's documentaries—their questioning of institutional authority—and especially his 1968 *High School*.

It wasn't at all clear to me what this piece was about until I was going over it with my *New Yorker* editor, Roger Angell (who wrote the title). He kept trying to make me explain what I was doing so we could improve the end, and in the course of a rambling excuse for what was already on the page, I blurted out the words "Alternative History," and he said, "That's it!"

WHAT HAPPENED

September 29, 1986

Dear:

We are fine. Please do not worry about us. I know it must have come as a shock to find your wife and children gone when you got home from work, but there is nothing to worry about. We are still the same loving family we were before. Nothing has changed. I will send you a post-office box number where we can be reached just as soon I know where we'll be, but at this point I don't know when that will be. All I can say is that any concern or anxiety on your part would be premature and alarmist.

Still, I know you can't help asking yourself: What happened? And the answer is: Nothing. Doc hung a curveball a couple of times, that's all. It could happen to anyone. There's no more to it than that. The Mets are still a winning team. What matters now is to take things one day at a time.

Please try to understand that although nothing has changed, nothing can stay exactly the same, either. No sane person could possibly have expected Doc to sustain the incredible greatness of last year. To expect that would be to expect superhuman perfection. Even Doc himself would admit that. But it's no reason to suspect that there's some hidden explanation for why things don't seem to be going as well as they used to (which doesn't mean things have changed, just that they're not going as well). Knowing you, I can tell that your mind is already racing with all sorts of gloomy scenarios based on little things that have happened in the past and now, in retrospect, loom as significant—like the ankle sprain before spring training. Believe me, I have searched my heart about the possibility that maybe the ankle sprain (without my even consciously realizing it) might have something to do with this, and I feel it's highly unlikely. Also, I hope you won't be tempted to dwell on some distressing generalization like "overthrowing" (because there is no such thing). I pray that other people won't encourage you in this line of thinking. There's always someone who will play on your nerves by saying, This is not as good as it was yesterday, so there must be something wrong. When, in fact, that's a contradiction. If anything, there's reason to think the opposite. If things are not as good as they were yesterday, isn't that all the more reason to believe that chances are they will be better next time? Especially for a young man with Dwight Gooden's extraordinary poise.

Now, dear, I want to confess something that I'm sure you're unaware of. For the past few months, every night after you've fallen asleep, I've been going downstairs and watching hundreds of hours of videotapes comparing Doc's pitching motion last year and this year. I didn't tell you about this, because I didn't want to upset you. But you know what I discovered? There is absolutely no difference! It's just that now he's not getting as many batters out. In other words, this is a more *mature* Doc. That's all I'm trying to explain.

But I can just hear you saying, What is the problem, then? Why has she gone away with the children and refused to tell me where she is? I can assure you with every bone in my body that there is no problem. Last year was the greatest year I've ever known, and I feel confident that future years will fulfill that potential, which may necessitate a few minor adjustments in Doc's mechanics, something that a number of qualified people are helping him with. Above all, I beg you not to pin any blame on Mel Stottlemyre, who doesn't even know us.

There's one thing I'm sure of. If you really have something, then almost by definition there are going to be certain times when you don't have it. If I didn't believe that, I wouldn't be so convinced that at this very moment you and I are closer than any two people could possibly be. Someday we'll look back on all this and, with the complex understanding that comes from placing great demands upon ourselves, we'll be able to say, It was nothing.

—Love,
KAY

P.S.: And Doc? He's better than ever.

SUMMER 1986

One day Sandy came over and we took some beers to Central Park and sat around talking about a cultural figure of the moment, Karen Finley, a performance artist who did shocking things like putting canned sauerkraut on her bare breasts. One article about her described this act as the breaking of a "taboo," and Sandy said, "*What* taboo? Since when is putting sauerkraut on your breasts taboo? Sleeping with your sister is taboo. Putting sauerkraut on your breasts is just—They don't say, '*We'd rather* you didn't sleep with your sister.' "

The other person everybody in New York was preoccupied with was Dwight Gooden, the Mets' star pitcher, twenty-one-year-old Doctor K. He hadn't been living up to his great 1985 season (24–4, Cy Young Award, led league in strikeouts); there was a vague perception that something was "wrong" with him, and a strong counterneed to suppress that perception. For a time, that need had the status of a genuine taboo. Doc's powers were almost mystically beloved by the fans and press. We wanted to know, but we needed not to know. My chief memory of that season (in which the Mets eventually won the Series) is of a gradual, reluctant surfacing of the question "What's the matter with Doc?" When it first occurred to me to write about this, I had a that-would-be-BAD feeling that gave me an almost sexual thrill: like, Oooooh, another woman's boyfriend! The thrill wasn't at being mean to Doc but at saying, We've been living in a dream world. Saying that seemed naughty.

Reading the sports pages was like Kremlinology. E.g., the *News:*

> [5/23] Giants . . . pummeled Gooden. . . . "It's strange," Gooden said . . . "after the fourth inning I started losing something. I think the temperature changed during the game. It was nice and sunny at first." . . . [6/3] Remember when 10-strikeout games were commonplace for the Doctor? All that has changed. Doc now is willing to settle for groundouts. He has learned that it is a lot easier on his arm. . . . [7/10] "He wasn't out there long enough to get into his game plan," said pitching coach Mel Stottlemyre. "A couple of balls fell in the holes, the next thing you know, it's 4–0. But I'm not worried about Dwight Gooden," Stottlemyre said for the thousandth time this season.

Two days later, Peter Schjeldahl (whose family—wife Brooke, daughter Ada—is always on the cutting edge of Mets-mania) called and said, "So what's your theory about Dwight?" I didn't have one, but he did: "There's something we're not being told—something very specific." (Good all-purpose theory.) This flavor of living amid propaganda inspired me to try doing a piece with drawings of International Doc News.

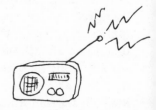

"General Pinochet announced

Pretoria

Nanagua

Moscow

Oh, well—I was losing heart for the story anyway. By late July it was starting to seem depressing, as if Doc might have some real arm problem.

Then Nicholas von Hoffman started egging me on. He had just moved to New York to research his book on Roy Cohn, and had gotten caught up in the local obsessions; almost every morning he'd call and tell me which newspapers to buy for the best Doc material. What finally prompted me to write was the wishful thinking in a late-August *News* headline, "DOC DELIVERS" (for a lackluster performance), and a dread that in the season's closing weeks the tantalizing story might slip away.

My boyfriend was in California on a long work trip, and I'd been feeling kind of resentful that he was gone all the time, so the Doc propaganda became a spouse's irrational explanation for leaving home. Some of the tortured reasoning about things being better next time came from a newspaper column on the business economy, but I forget which one.

The *New Yorker* couldn't run the story for a couple of weeks; I wanted to root for Doc, but didn't want him to be so good that he'd ruin my story. Then the Mets came up with another spectacular rationalization (for a costly three-run homer Doc gave up to the Giants): (1) It was just the one pitch; (2) the pitch itself wasn't that bad; (3) the batter just happened to be looking for that pitch.

At the time, there was something exhilarating about slightly relaxing our grip on the illusion of perfection. But the next spring was the spring of "GOODEN AGREES TO TREATMENT AFTER A TEST SHOWS DRUG USE." He seems fine now.

HANDS UP

The President . . . often repeat[s] tales of how
much individual farmers get from the federal
government. When [an aide] told Reagan recently
that a California farmer got $12 million, the
president put his hands over his face and said,
"What are we doing wrong?"

—*The* New Republic, *February 16, 1987*

One of the worst things you can do is touch your hands to
your face—especially the eyes, nose, and mouth; you are giving household staphylococcus germs a free ride. Always
avoid touching any part of the face whatsoever with bare
hands, as this will just work the stain deeper into the skin
and allow it to "set," making it difficult or impossible to re-
move even with coarse abrasives. Never, under any circumstances, cover the face with the hands. Doing so will not only
cut off the supply of fresh oxygen and clog the vents but will
block the audience's sight lines as well as those of any down-
stage members of the cast. Using your hands to conceal your
face is strictly against the rules unless you are already the one
wearing the blindfold. Be sure not to put both hands over the
face while operating a tractor, cultivator, or weed eater. This
is really asking for trouble, because in many non-Western
cultures the gesture means something quite different, and
could make you conspicuous or even give somebody the
wrong idea. Drawing out the poison will then be that much
harder to do if access to the face is blocked by the hands, and

you will be in a blind spot where the assault team cannot pick up your signal. It is a violation of military courtesy to return a salute by raising the hands and positioning them on the face, even as an empty formality. Taking cover is sometimes a necessity, but the hands should always allow the eyes to distinguish the living from the dead, the nose to detect noxious toxins, and the mouth to admit nourishing fresh-grown produce from the local bivouac area. Although a man running rapidly toward a bank does furnish a poor target, do not forget that tellers are forbidden by statute from releasing funds to anyone whose face is concealed by hands.

These fundamental warnings and strictures all too often go unheeded, thanks to the widespread failure to comprehend that once the hands are placed directly onto the face, they can stick there. Or they can even go right through. Sometimes they come out at the back of the head; sometimes they don't. For many, these risks exert a deadly attraction. Casually the hands are lifted, and then, almost before anyone knows what has happened, the hands have settled upon the face. It's dark in there. Cool and dark. Everything suddenly seems so simple. For a while. But after a while, faraway and tantalizing, comes a sound. The idea of a sound touching against the idea of another sound. What is it—a Japanese wind chime?

Don't do it. Don't even think about it.

FEBRUARY 1987

Adam Gopnik had a story scheduled to run in the *New Yorker*'s Anniversary Issue, which was the last issue Mr. Shawn had edited, and I was trying to bump it out with something topical they'd be forced to run right away. (I liked Adam a lot, and his story, "The Blue Room," was lovely, but I didn't want it to be in that issue at that moment in *New Yorker* history. Bob Gottlieb had just been put in as editor and had brought Adam with him from Knopf—so Adam willy-nilly stood for the new regime.)

The quote about Reagan was in the current *New Republic*. I free-associated for one day, and then told myself to dream more material—actually dreamed the wind chimes. The next day brought one of those lucky coincidences—my trusty infantry manual happened to open to a page about "taking cover." Determined to make some kind of piece, fast, I threw in anything—didn't care about repeating myself with this grab-bag of phrases merged into a surreal surface. Didn't even care what I stole: Frederick Barthelme, one of the writers I was editing, is also one of the funniest improvisational talkers, so I called him in Mississippi and said, "Hi, Rick, I'm writing a piece about all the terrible things that can happen if you cover your face with your hands. Any ideas?" He said, "They could go right through," and then he said, "It's dark in there," and I copied it all down. Meanwhile I was trying to force another writer to submit a story in case mine didn't work out. Neither of us beat the deadline.

Whatever idea lay behind this piece was so intuitive I had zero sense of how it would come across. I've never written anything else where I was equally prepared to hear it was horrible or great. After turning it in, I had an appalling flashback to a newspaper photo of Mr. Shawn, just after being forced to resign, leaving the Algonquin Hotel with his hands shielding his face from the camera—and thought, Oh, God, did I subconsciously write this about *that*? Maybe I should take it back. . . . Asked a colleague whose judgment I respected, who said it was paranoid to think anyone would make the connection, and if they did—well, I'd just blend in with all the other people who were behaving insanely out of distress at what was happening to the *New Yorker*. So I decided to trust that the piece had its own little self-contained rationale, which could be taken at face value.

MORE
UNWELCOME NEWS

The Air Force Logistics Command ordered its
spare-parts buyers to spend as much money as
possible in the last 10 days of 1985 because
appropriated funds are piling up faster
than the Air Force is using them,
according to defense officials.

—*The* Washington Post, *January 2, 1986*

At the House Foreign Affairs Committee . . . it got
downright poetic. . . . Waxing eloquent about the
ingratitude of all peoples toward their military
forces in peacetime, [Rep. Robert] Dornan
paraphrased Rudyard Kipling's poem "Tommy
Atkins." . . . Rep. Mervyn Dymally . . . shot back
with a little cautionary verse from Shakespeare.

—*The New York* Daily News, *December 10, 1986*

It was peacetime: Tuesday, December 31, 1985. And it was
lunchtime. But as Air Force purchasing specialist Major Jim
Spender left his desk and wedged himself into the elevator
with the midday crowd leaving early for New Year's Eve, his
mind was uneasy. A piece of paper was burning a hole in his
pocket: a procurement memo from his boss, dated December
20, ordering him to spend $50,000 on spare parts by the end
of the month—or else!

During the past week and a half, he had worked heroi-
cally to meet the deadline, but much of his time had been

consumed just trying to think of unusual spare parts that no one else in the command might have thought of ordering already. He knew his colleagues had all received the same memo, and there was intense competitiveness over who could come up with more orders for spare parts that other people hadn't realized the need for. That first day when the memo came down, he had really lucked out. He was doing deep-breathing exercises in the hall outside his office—a technique he had read about in a CIA psych. ops. manual called *Breath Control and Guerrilla Warfare*, whose lessons he had adapted to relax his mind and visualize obscure spare parts. As he was exercising, he accidentally hit the wall thermostat with one arm, knocking off the clear plastic cover. When he stooped to pick it up, he saw that he had also knocked off and then stepped on a small, circular piece of brushed chrome that served as a decorative concealment over the mechanism of the temperature indicator, and was now slightly bent out of shape.

Quickly he replaced the plastic cover (so nobody would notice the thermostat and get any bright ideas), took the damaged part into his office, whipped a requisition form off the stack on his desk, and typed in a description: "Disk, ornamental, chrome, brushed, thermostat." Mindful of the memo's warning that haste should not override "constraints of law, directives, prudence, and bona fide need rules," he did not try to inflate the cost but neatly divided the part's square footage into the market value of an F-111, tacked on the minimum 300 percent for "Miscellaneous Closing Costs (Estimated)" and sent his secretary scurrying down to Processing with the requisition.

Well and good—but the thermostat coup had used up only $49,000 of his quota. In all honesty he could not have justified ordering more than twelve gross of the disks. So he still had a grand to get rid of, and now he would have to work overtime on New Year's Eve. He glanced at the pile of catalogues on his desk. Spiegel, Sporty's Tool Shop, Touch of Class . . . he had long ago picked them clean for spare-parts ideas. He had even ordered cable TV for his office, at his own expense, to get Home Shopping Network, but whenever he watched it they were offering gold or sterling neck chains—just the whole chain, no parts. He wondered what these people did who ordered nothing but a chain and then broke a link or a catch and were stuck without the proper replacement part at hand. He supposed they let it lie around unused in the back of a dresser drawer, or took it some distance from home to a repair middleman who made them wait weeks and weeks until the requisite part came in from a wholesaler. He ruminated on the terrible wastage that typified American life.

As the elevator finally released him he was still deep in meditation, and began to patrol the network of Pentagon hallways, his "ALL AREAS" clearance badge flapping gently against his breast pocket and rendering his almost trancelike movements smoothly unbroken even at security checkpoints. When he had first come to work in the famous five-sided building, he had been warned against getting lost. But now he wanted to get lost, so lost that his mental rhythm would drift loose of the rigid, prosaic syntax that had too long constricted it: wing, airplane, aluminum. . . .

After a time (later on he would not be able to remember how long a time, or what route he took) he found himself in a strange concourse of little shops. What appeared to have once been an attractive, bustling arcade—drugstore, passport photos, hosiery—was now a deserted row of tarnished-brass storefronts, half-obliterated signs, dust-clouded display windows: an economic doom, he guessed, wrought by the labyrinthine architecture of the very place that was begging its employees to spend money.

Yet even as he thought this, he saw that one shop door

stood ajar. A crudely lettered cardboard sign hanging from the doorknob read "AUCTION GALERIA—ANTIQUES."

As he stepped inside, overgrown fern tendrils brushed his face; for a moment he caught the sickening, slightly sweet aroma of cheap potting soil. Stacked C-ration cases towered to the ceiling. In the doorway to a back room, beaded strings formed a bizarre curtain, dangling in the humid air. A macaw screeched at him from its perch.

"May I to show you something especial?" The man who parted the curtain spoke with a slight accent. Major Spender could not place it, but he noted the American boots and hand-me-down National Security Council sweatshirt favored by operatives of the Nicaraguan Contras' counterintelligence service. The man held a tin mess-kit plate filled with tiny blue chili peppers. "Small snack," he said apologetically, and extended the plate to his customer. "Please be joining me." But the mere sight of the chilies seared the major's throat, and he declined with a smile.

Briefly, the man dropped his eyes to Major Spender's clearance badge, on which "PURCHASING" could be clearly read. "I let you have some beautiful TOW antitank missiles," he said. "Guaranteed offensive capability, merely five thousand dollar each."

The major explained that his budget was unfortunately limited to $1,000 and that anyway he was just looking.

"Many valuable wrenches and toilet seats," said the man in a sly, insinuating tone. "On sale, five hundred each, definite antiques."

The major guessed he was being teased—a ritual test before sincere negotiation could take place. To show good faith, he bought one of the seats (which did look very old), wrote out a Pentagon chit, and then said he was looking for more unusual parts. "Something out of the ordinary."

"I have maybe one such rarity," said the man. "My assistant will bring." He raised his voice to a shriek: "Ronquita!"

Abruptly the curtain parted; listening on the other side the whole time must have been this gorgeous Latino girl. She wore a sarong made from parachute silk, secured at the waist with a belt braided from what looked like the paper strips the major had seen in the Pentagon shredder room. Slung across her shoulder was an M-16. The man noticed Major Spender's surprised glance at the weapon and remarked casually, "For cosmetic purposes solely. Many shoplifters." The girl stood there, impassive, sullenly scratching her trigger finger. Then the man barked an order in Spanish. She went into the back room and brought out a Maxwell House coffee can. Prying off the plastic lid, she took out a small sheet of yellowed paper and laid it for display on one of the C-ration cases.

"A most interesting curiosa," said the man.

Major Spender bent over to peer at the paper. On it was a single line of old-looking handwriting—"Unwelcome news, nipping like a frost, making soldiers hang their heads"—surrounded by doodles and crossed-out stuff. The major's heart pounded. He recognized the line at once as unmistakably the work of William Shakespeare. It was staggeringly obvious that the Bard's characteristic diction and imagery were stamped on every word. It was obvious because Major Spender, with no formal training as an Elizabethan scholar, was nonetheless an expert in parts. Show him a part and he could instantly extrapolate the whole. He saw exactly how this line, with its crudely exposed nuts and bolts of language, would slot smoothly into an overall assembly by means of mechanisms unique to the Swan of Avon; how the line's configuration of incompleteness dictated other lines it must interlock with to form scenes and acts, plots and themes, all functioning as a single magnificent machine. Nor did he have the slightest reason to doubt that the writing was Shakespeare's own hand.

Guardedly, he murmured a noncommital "Hmm."

"You have disappointment," said the man. "I am sorry."

He returned the paper to the coffee can. "We have other shop in basement of the White House. Perhaps there you are finding better bargains."

"No, wait," said the major. "Possibly it could come in handy. I'll give you five hundred for it."

"Ixnay on the humanitarian aid. Twenty million."

Major Spender was no loose cannon. "I don't have that kind of authorization," he said. "I'd have to go back to the office and get a special voucher. And it's New Year's Eve— I'm not even sure if anybody's still there right now. Can you hold it for me till after the holidays?"

He did not hear the answer, for in the next moment he did something the motive for which would forever baffle him. Maybe he was afraid he sounded weak and vacillating. Maybe he was just adventuristically proving his machismo to Ronquita, who was contemptuously fiddling with the safety on her M-16. Or maybe he sincerely wanted to help his country. He suddenly reached out and took one of the chili peppers, and popped it into his mouth.

When he came to, back in his office, his upper respiratory system felt blowtorched and his desk was littered with paper cups from the water cooler. He could not remember drinking the water, or his return route, or anything else following the fateful pepper. The emergency-call light on his phone was blinking.

"*Bueno!*" said a hysterical voice when he picked up. It was Commander Zero, the White House switchboard operator. "Nobody is answering there. Now we have a big push here to wrap up the Ironside Project *pronto*. We are missing one vital part. Just a line of dialogue we are needing for Act Two, Scene Four, a military scene. I can't tell you the plot— it's classified—but we have 'IRONSIDE colon' and then we need 'Da-da da-da, da da-da da-da, da da-da da-da da-da.' You can scrounge something? Whatever fits good—we can plug it in and be ready for to roll."

Major Spender said he would get right on it.

"It is a nipping and a vicious breeze," he scribbled frantically on a pad. No, that wasn't it. "Air nips, methinks, if soldiers think it so. Nippingly, hounds of news do bring bad air. The frost nips like a dog and icy news laps at the soldiers' faces like a tongue. It is a nipsome and a chilly news. The hangdog news doth nip, unwelcome beast."

He thought he had the gist of it. But with a precisely tooled part like this, "gist" was a contradiction in terms. *Damn it,* he thought, *I'm a purchasing specialist, not an iambics engineer.* Despairingly, he put his head in his hands. *If only I'd been able to give that Contra the twenty million. . . .*

But "if only" is a concept with no relevance to the geopolitical struggle for total dominance in the field of Shakespeare studies. And so it was that New Year's, 1986, saw a new and dangerous tilt in the balance of power.

LONDON—A former civil servant claims he has conclusive evidence that a play entitled *Edmund Ironside* was actually written by William Shakespeare. . . . It predates the first recognized Shakespeare play, *Titus Andronicus.* . . . The claim . . . came a month after an American scholar at Oxford said he had identified a new poem by the Bard. . . .

" 'Unwelcome news, nipping like a frost, making soldiers hang their heads'—that kind of idea and that kind of phraseology is in both plays. It cannot be coincidence."

—*United Press International, January 2, 1986*

These are only the facts that have come out so far, from Major Spender's testimony before the investigating committee. I find these revelations mind-boggling. It defies credulity that the White House could be running a covert Shakespeare-scholarship operation if even switchboard-rank officers knew about it. Also, it's hard to swallow that if the Contra group in the Pentagon basement had the original manuscript, the exact same thing somehow ended up a day or two later in the hands of a third country, England. And if it fit in a "coffee can," where did the rest of the play come from? Furthermore, without wanting to assign credibility where none has so far been proved, it is inconceivable that not one single person in the Administration ever took the responsibility of stepping forward to inquire if the international English-poetry trade was being manipulated by foreign zealots on the President's staff. In any case, even if one accepts that global domination of Shakespeare studies is a legitimate foreign-policy objective, this is an extremely curious way to go about it.

It is excellent that the investigation has already brought so much information to light. But there must be facts that have not come out yet.

ALL OF 1986

In January, 1986, in Florida, the same issue of the St. Petersburg *Times* ran those two items—about surplus Air Force appropriations and an alleged discovery of a Shakespeare play—and I turned them into a straightforward, silly story about an Air Force purchasing specialist who finds a bogus Shakespeare manuscript in a derelict antique shop in the Pentagon basement. The *New Yorker* bounced it back, saying they didn't see any logical reason for Shakespeare to be in it. Six months later, a *Times* item, "EX-OFFICERS ACCUSE CONTRA CHIEFS OF SIPHONING OFF U.S. AID MONEY," inspired me to turn the antique shop into a Contra money-making scam being run in the Pentagon basement. Another rejection: Still not funny. Sent it to Roy Blount to see if he had any pointers, and got back a postcard of detailed suggestions, beginning, "Assuming we are not at war by the time it comes out, I think it takes too long to get to the twist."

In November, the Iran-Contra deal blew open. I had predicted it! If the *New Yorker* had run my story, they would have looked brilliant! *Uh-ohhh, now she thinks she's psychic. . . .* (Of course, the North-Poindexter crowd later denied that their offices were in the White House "basement." The press must have gotten that word from the same cliché pool I did.) I rewrote the thing with new details about TOW antitank missiles, etc., and got another rejection: Still not funny, Shakespeare still baffling. Michael Kinsley almost bought it for the *New Republic* but said the surplus-appropriations hook was hackneyed press fodder, a pseudostory that comes out every year. (Yes, he's the same guy who encouraged me to attack Pentagon overspending in the dog-boarding case. Typical of him to distinguish between a legitimate target and a trumped-up one.) I like a rejection based on superior expertise, so gave up on the story. Then in December the Congressmen on the House Foreign Affairs Committee, investigating Iranscam, started quoting Kipling *and Shakespeare* at each other. Success at last!—just add a few references to that, resubmit . . . But no—now the Shakespeare was "overexplained and no longer funny."

GQ printed it with a quintessential magazine illustration—a yellow-and-red drawing of a parrot and a Contra temptress, which really suited the trashiness of the storytelling. Maybe the deconstructionists are right about the dread seductions of narrative; it was like a railroad train I couldn't get off. As it hurtled forward, I glimpsed with envy a brief, elegant comment in a letter from Lynn Caraganis: "On the news last night they said George Bush announced he had 'protested in private about McFarlane's trip to Iran.' He may have said something like, 'How come Bud gets to go via Switzerland?' "

POLL

Which of these descriptions do you feel describe
Lieut. Colonel North?

SOMEONE I WOULD WANT TO MARRY MY DAUGHTER

Describes	*Does not describe*	*Not sure*
26%	57%	17%

—*From a poll cited in* Time

Dad doesn't know this, and he's going to be furious when he finds out, but I think Oliver North is the guy who married my sister. I can't be a hundred percent sure, but I would describe him as such, and I'm almost positive it was the same guy. (If you already have a predisposition to accept this, or are willing to take my word for it, don't even bother to read on. Just call 1-900-555-TRUE to have your vote tabulated immediately. There is a fifty-cent charge for each call.) He was going under the name Bobby George North back then, but I recognize the personality structure. During the time all this happened, around 1984–85, my sister was living down in Cocoahole, Florida, and kept the marriage a secret from the family, but was constantly calling me long-distance to tell me about this guy she was seeing, Bobby George North, and how he was driving her crazy with his manipulations, cheating on her and then sweet-talking her when she got mad. (If you find these facts, including names, dates, and places, to be plausible so far, please don't hesitate to organize a group of friends to send large numbers of supportive telegrams to me, c/o Western Union.) He was always telling her he had to go to Miami on business, and then he'd stay away for days or weeks, and when he came back he'd order her not to question him about his business and then he'd butter her up some more. I started trying to get her to break up with him and come stay with me in New York until she got over him (and if you think that gives me some personal motive, casting doubt on my credibility, simply call 1-900-555-HMMM to register your temporary suspension of judgment at this time until you have finished reading this and weighed all the evidence), but she said that Bobby George was in many ways a little boy and he needed her. (Do you have the feeling that I'm basically an honest person? I know you can't answer that for certain, but do you get a general sense of probity and forthrightness from the way I express myself?

YES_____   NO_____

Don't forget to put a check mark or, preferably, your initials in the appropriate space, then clip and send to CBS News Poll, New York, New York 10019.)

Now, the rest of what I know I only learned after it was all over and my sister told me the whole truth. In the fall of 1984, she finally gave Bobby George an ultimatum, because she was pregnant, so they went to the Community Gardens Church and got married. She says they never got any papers proving they were married, and she now suspects that it wasn't a real church and Bobby George had just staged the whole thing by renting a building and hiring some drifters to decorate it like a church and pose as ministers. (If this sounds mind-boggling, is there some other explanation you could come up with that would account for her not having the papers? If so, why not take a few moments to jot it down and send it to the *Washington Post,* Op-Ed Page, Washington, D.C. 20071.) To make a long story short, the marriage changed nothing, and Bobby George persisted in his bad behavior even after my sister gave birth to her baby. (Do you believe me now? Even if you feel you've already answered the question, that was a few sentences ago, so keep in mind that you retain the option at any time to call 1-900-555-TRUE to register the complexity of your views as the shifting winds and erosions of public opinion alter your perception of reality.) Finally, sometime in February 1985, Bobby George said he would drive my sister and the baby to the pediatrician. On the way, he pulled up at a Pick Kwik, said he was just going to get a large container of coffee, snuck out the back door of the Pick Kwik, and went to a nearby Trailways bus station, where he'd checked his bags ahead of time. My sister never saw him again. Later it turned out that before he'd left the house he'd given the dog a dog sleeping-pill so it couldn't follow him, and it didn't wake up until the next day. (Note that this account reflects a four percent margin of error.)

If you are convinced by now that this story is worth pursuing further, even though I can't prove anything, or if you feel that the revelations herein do not provide you with sufficient information to decide whether or not it suggests a continuing and widespread pattern of abuse, including the possibility that this North was the same duplicitous lover-boy who took advantage of *your* sister and then dumped her, please take the trouble to form your own independent polling organization so that the proliferation of opinion may continue to flourish as it must in an open society. Thank you for your patience.

JULY 1987

Dan Menaker, who had an office next to mine and was funny to be around, once gave me the idea to use 1-800 numbers in something. I was working on this:

MIND POLICE

If you care to register disagreement with anything I say, please call the following number: 1-800-URWRONG. The F.C.C. requires that these stupid numbers be inserted throughout everything I say. I ask you—1-800-IANSWER—what better evidence could there be of the totalitarian mentality?

The most important thing in preserving the integrity of your opinion is not to hang out beforehand with anybody who might interfere with what you think. This is the advice I give younger opinion makers, but few of them take it to heart. They will go out for drinks with people who completely disagree with me, and then I'm forced to stand up and be counted.

Don't they realize I have my own independent system for dealing with differences of opinion? Everyone is free to write to me; then I read the letters and have a good, hearty laugh at their expense. Sometimes I read the letters aloud to colleagues, like [funny name], who often drops by my office and sits on the couch all hunched over with his thumbs in his pants cuffs so I won't be able to tell if he's going Thumbs Up or Thumbs Down.

He always ends up agreeing with me, but his thumbs are smaller and thicker than mine, so the shape of his argument is always quite different. For years I've tried to get him a post somewhere else where he'd really loosen up the stuffy Peter-Pan-collar atmosphere that's everywhere, but no dice. There is still tremendous prejudice in the opinion industry against anyone perceived as a protégé of mine. It's their loss. 1-800-ITISNOT.

Then Oliver North started testifying at the Iran-Contra hearings, most of which I listened to in the office on a bulky old portable radio of Dan's. (It had the improbable brand name "Lloyd's" and had done political-scandal duty in the fiction department for years.) When North boasted about his stacks of telegrams and then the news media turned into one big moment-to-moment poll of his popularity, the 1-800 joke had to be pressed into immediate service. (It got changed to 1-900 because those cost 50 cents per call, and I wanted people to pay through the nose for succumbing to opinion madness.)

There was a nagging technical problem of how to get from the *Time* poll, with the fathers who did or didn't want their daughters to marry North, to the two sisters I wanted to write about. These tiny obstacles are the ones that make you blank out and almost give up. Then I ran into Adam Gopnik in the hall and babbled my problem, and he said instantly, " 'Dad's gonna be so mad when he finds out. . . .' "

This was fun to write. An implausible narrative full of excuses for why it doesn't exactly sound convincing is an easy form. You can keep commenting spontaneously on your own inept storytelling. Also, I got to write about Florida again. While trying to sell our house there, my brother and I had been in a pursuit-and-evasion car chase with the lawyer for a buyer who was stalling; we finally caught up with him at a Pick Kwik, where he bought coffee and acted skillfully lackadaisical: "Oh, yah, the papers, sure." Family vs. legal duplicity—that was the feeling for the story.

My AND ED'S PEACE PROPOSALS

Ed and I each have come up with a proposed plan for the cessation of hostilities between the Reagan Administration and our household. Since our plans differ in certain minor respects (Ed taking a somewhat tougher line), we offer both versions, in the hope that they may at least stimulate the Administration to consider negotiations toward ending the past six and a half years of drawn-out mutual aggression and mistrust. This is not a ploy or a farce on our part. We are even putting all our personal problems on the back burner while we press these initiatives. We now task the Administration with showing how sincere *it* is by responding in a spirit of reconciliation and good faith.

MY PLAN

1. Immediate suspension of Elliott Abrams, who will then be reflagged as a Kuwaiti vessel.

2. Unconditional withdrawal of the Bork nomination; Bork allowed to head a Presidential commission on the colorization of film classics.

ED'S PLAN

1. Ed given a line-item veto on Presidential rhetoric.

2. Immediate amnesty for Ed's mother, a political prisoner of right-wing mailing lists.

3. Trade and assistance: As soon as the first two conditions are met, we will give support to the Administration's economic goals by ceasing our costly flow of Mailgrams to the White House, thus freeing funds for disbursement to more productive sectors of the economy and enabling us to stop accepting aid from Ed's mother.

4. National plebiscite on secular humanism, to be supervised by elected representatives from four regional productions of *La Cage aux Folles*.

5. Timetable for routine Rorschach and Stanford-Binet testing of President Reagan.

3. U.S. diplomatic relations with puppet regime of Pat Buchanan severed for an indefinite cooling-off period; in return, Ed will use all his influence to halt Latin-American incursions by Joan Didion.

4. Arms reduction: Ronald Reagan to enter into a one-on-one dialogue with Peter Ueberroth to achieve a 60-day suspension of Mike Scott of the Houston Astros for pitching defaced baseballs. This is just to give Ed an added incentive to abide by the remainder of the plan.

5. Timetable for the election of someone else as President by the end of 1988.

AUGUST 1987

Written on jury duty. As my fellow jurors saw me going through the *New York Times*, underlining things adjacent to photos of Daniel Ortega and making numbered lists on a legal pad, they must have thought I was a serious student of the peace process. Reagan's proposals didn't seem serious, so the situation seemed to call for another strategic use of the Ed couple, with their self-serving idealism. And the Column A versus Column B format in the *Times* was a new structure to play around with.

Dan Menaker reminded me of a great phrase that had come up in the Iran-Contra hearings: "task with." General Secord, for instance, had been tasked with certain things. High time this usage entered standard English.

When the piece came out, a lot of friends told me they liked the Elliott Abrams joke. It's kind of a bad-Carson-monologue joke, but why should we liberals be more fastidious than Abrams? I'm sorry I didn't put in an Orrin Hatch joke. I was writing for people who shared all the same beefs and wanted to see them listed with absolutely no sense of proportion.

PAT ROBERTSON'S CATALOGUE ESSAY FOR A NEW EXHIBITION OF PAINTINGS BY DAVID SALLE

> Mr. Robertson had . . . a dramatic religious experience. . . . "I walked across a curtain to a whole new life," he says now. "I understood why I was here, I understood my purpose, I even understood modern art."
>
> —The Wall Street Journal, *October 6, 1987*

1

Here is a young painter who may be said to represent the finest traditions of the University of London Graduate School Art Appreciation Program and the Christian Broadcasting Network School of Fine Arts, and if that is not word for word what it says on his résumé provided by the Mary Boone Gallery, under whose caring aegis this show takes place, who are we to let a few minutiae distract us from the powerful statements in the other 99 percent of these colossal paintings?

For here is a young man whose controversial work cries

out to us for understanding. Let us rise above his minor details, let us open our hearts to what he might be trying to tell us, let us see how even the titles of his paintings speak to us as in tongues on our own pain and life experiences. *The Wildness of Oats. How Many Miles Is It to the Combat Zone? Now Another Distortion. Sharks in a Feeding Frenzy.*

But my goodness gracious, how the supersophisticated have hounded him with their criticisms. How they look down their noses every time he traces something. Yes indeed, he has traced the figure of the front-line soldier in *Combat Zone* from a war comic. And I say to you, does the Lord distinguish between the love that a man puts into tracing something faithfully to the way his Maker caused it to be made and the love that another man puts into drawing something from his own God-given imagination or rendering it freehand the way it appears to him in the light that the Almighty created on the First Day? Is not tracing just as much an act of commitment and obedience? For is not repetition equally, if not more so, an act of faith and humility? Amen. And did the Lord not make not only the soldier alive and in his foxhole but also the war comic and the very newsstand whereat the war comic is sold, and is it not just as much an example of the workings of Divine Grace if a man, also himself created by God, comes along and buys the war comic and then later casts it into the gutter, whereupon along comes this young David, with his eye on the same gutter, and singles out the war comic from amid the useless rubble of stones?

2

It makes me ashamed, as David's fellow man, to bring up the media's cruel attack on these paintings, which are many feet high and wide, as nothing more than behemoth party invitations. Yes, there are surely parties in the art world, and at those parties there is liquor. Yes, a handful of people may say to themselves, "David is going to be at the party, so count me in, and the Devil take the hindmost!" But to conclude, as some have done, that this young man bears the burden of responsibility for all the liquor consumption in the art world, to say his true vocation is that of "liquor courier," is an unfair calumny unless you can prove it.

Furthermore, let us pause and ask ourselves just why it is that we Americans expect our artists and their dealers, friends, and collectors to hold to a higher standard of morality than the rest of us.

3

Now, there are other people who honestly and without hypocrisy raise a moral issue that is a little more legitimate. These people would look at this series of works called *Nudes: 19:12–29* and find it sinful to paint the figure of a woman naked, in all the many postures of temptation on a Colonial settee of the type that might be found in a Christian home, and then to apply washes of dark colors that make it hard to see the truth of Divinely created flesh—and not only that, but then to glue onto each canvas some household object so dreadful that it would not be tolerated in any Christian home, thus most selfishly diverting the viewer's eye from the woman's God-given minor details.

I know the people who cannot appreciate this kind of art. They are loving people. I know that because I have been there myself. But then I searched my soul, and behold, I found that extra bit of compassion that allowed me to say, "David, I understand." And that is why I have come to believe that this young man has earned a place on the list with Albers, Arp, Balla, Beckmann, Boccioni, and so on. Like these other moderns, he prompts us to the highest response that we, as good people, can give to the works of our fellow man: Forgiveness.

OCTOBER 1987

One day a clipping arrived in the mail: the Pat Robertson quote, with its theological anticlimax, "I even understood modern art." Written on it was a note—"Your kind of prose"—from Joel Conarroe. (He should know—he used to be head of the Modern Language Association of America.) This was a discerning gift and an irresistible premise. I called Sandy to tell him about it, and that I was going to write it up as an analysis of David Salle's paintings. Sandy said, "Why don't you do it as Pat Robertson's Guide to the Galleries? That way you could get a lot more stuff in." This was an instance of counterhelp—a suggestion that usefully polarizes you to what you really want to do. The strength of my resistance to his idea told me something. Having an excuse to write about Salle was exciting. People in New York didn't sit around talking about what was at the galleries; they sat around talking about whether David Salle was any good. You had to have an opinion. But I didn't know what I thought. *Mmmm, trouble.* Also, I'd met Salle at the Schjeldahls' and liked him (he had an unusual laugh, like a cough), so there was another *frisson* of trouble—wondering whether he'd be annoyed at what I wrote.

The previous winter I'd seen his paintings for the first time, at the Whitney Museum. They were big, they were full of references to other pictures, and they were cryptic in a nerve-racking way, like "asking about how do I envision probably the getting together of the two Koreas." They just seemed like too much trouble. *What—I have to deal with all this now?* Then, in the spring, a show of watercolors—all variations on one idea: a nude with weird little images superimposed. These were easier to take in, and I thought, Well, maybe this was an obvious road to go down and nobody else had the guts to go down it because it seemed too obvious. I asked Peter Schjeldahl about this, and he said, "Other painters have done it, but none of them have done it with his concentration. It's like, he builds a car and leaves out the engine—*and it runs anyway.*" I repeated this in a conversation with Adam Gopnik, and he said, "The reason it runs is because people like you and Peter Schjeldahl are running along underneath, carrying it."

I didn't have a coherent way of thinking about these paintings, but the attacks on them as cynical image-playback didn't seem right. I'd played back some images myself, and in fact what had initially exhausted me in Salle's work was its earnestness; it seemed to demand that I kitty up an equal amount of the same. And now Pat Robertson was demanding "forgiveness" and "compassion" for "a few minor details" (premarital sex, exaggerated credentials as a "tax lawyer" and University of London "graduate student," and a distorted claim to "combat service" in Korea. One source had described his wartime job as "liquor courier." On *Nightline* Robertson's idea of a sincere response was to redefine *all* of Korea as "a combat zone.") It seemed that Salle the Aesthetic Antichrist was about as profound a concept as Robertson the Spiritual Leader.

This mirror logic then dictated that if I gave Salle credit for moral decency, I had to give Robertson credit for art appreciation. He "understood modern art"—fine, so let him explicate these paintings for me. That was trouble, because I was writing double-blind, as ignorant of how Robertson's preaching would sound as of what could be said for Salle. Of course, I could have done research, but I wasn't interested in parodying Robertson or satirizing Salle. It was more fun and trouble to let a few shreds of information serve, and see where they would lead. All I had was "tracing" (had read somewhere that Salle traced certain images) and a generic sense of evangelical repetition. But you know, in a way, come to think of it, weren't they the same thing? Bluffing through a religious rationale for Salle's paintings, I started to feel convinced by my joke argument. (Told this to Peter, and he said, "Now you know what art critics do.")

My aim was to rise to the level of sophistication of the paintings, but I had no conviction about where that level was. (Sometimes pieces end up as pathetic souvenirs of your original ambitions.) And there's a comedy-writing inertia that's hard to keep resisting. (The "liquor courier" reference is opportunistic, and the reverse moralizing about naked women too easy.) But I was happy to be able to arrive at that one sentence about paintings I didn't understand: "David, I understand." I couldn't get there in my own voice, but I could as "Pat Robertson." When David Salle read the story, this process was all he saw—maybe because he'd never heard of Pat Robertson.

I didn't have any wider intentions, but in hindsight—here's a certain cultural situation. Here's this guy making his paintings, doing his job, and being lionized and chewed up by the art public; so he's getting millions of dollars, but if "Pat Robertson" has Christian compassion for him, why not? And the rest of us are under pressure to have an opinion about the art. The piece is just an artifact of pressure. After I wrote it, the pressure was off me, and I actually had an authentic response to the art, but what that was is irrelevant here.

A LOT
IN COMMON

On January 10, 1941, at Piedmont Hospital in Atlanta, my mother wrote in the space for my first name on my birth certificate: "Annabelle." She was from Philly, but went down South with my father when the Army assigned him to Fort McPherson, and she must have gotten carried away. When she snapped out of it, she renamed me for her younger sister Vera. My baby book, bound in pink cloth, *Our Baby's First Seven Years,* was a present from Aunt Vera, and still has her congratulations card pasted in it:

> May life bring *EVERY* joy to bless
> That tiny "dream of *HAPPINESS!*"

The book has a page for Baby's First Gifts, and my mother filled it in with her neat secretarial-school penmanship: "Bathinette—Granma. Toys—Granpa. Bunting—Aunt Vera. White wool shawl—Aunt Laura. Gold cross and chain—Ondine and Charlie O'Donnell. Baby hot water bottle—Mary Virginia Stealey. Gold heart necklace—Atlanta Q.M. Depot gang. Silver orange juice cup—Daddy. Sweater, cap, and booties—Mr. and Mrs. King (grocer). Piggie bank—Aunt Thelma." On the page for Favorite Toys, my mother wrote, "Horace the Horse" (a red stuffed horse with a white string mane). "At eleven months, Ronnie 'loved' it and sat on it." (I was nicknamed Ronnie so Aunt Vera wouldn't have to be Big Vera.)

. . .

When *Our Baby's First Seven Years* was full—when seven years' worth of physical development, food preferences, vocabulary growth, trips, and names of playmates had been duly organized, recorded, and put away—my life was on the brink of shapelessness, bereft of a unifying principle, vulnerable to any dangerous pattern that might come along and attach itself to my future in seven-year cycles of bad luck or a seventy-seven-year evil spell. But on that very day, my seventh birthday, January 10, 1948, someone I would meet thirty-five years later, a friend of mine named Donald, was born. This turn of fortune took place in a postwar New Jersey suburb, or maybe it was Brooklyn. His parents must have named him after the Hollywood song-and-dance man Donald O'Connor, who had been doing a series of low-budget Universal musicals as the juvenile lead opposite such starlets as Ann Blyth and was destined to make the Francis the Talking Mule movies.

. . .

Back in Philly, I celebrated many January 10ths with my best friend, Marie, whose parents owned a greeting-card shop. (After school, I'd help her put price tags on the cards with tiny oval clips, making fun of the verses—"May life bring *EVERY* joy to bless"—and then we'd go sit on a park bench and draw pictures of women wearing spike heels and those seamed stockings with squared-off reinforcements up the backs of the ankles.) One birthday she gave me a record album of fairy tales read by some actor; and whenever we listened to "Sleeping Beauty," as the Prince approached the briar hedge that had grown higher and higher till it covered the castle where lay the Princess in her hundred-year sleep, Marie would stop the record and intone, "He came to the edge of an impen—, an impen—, an impen—, an impenetrable forest."

. . .

On January 10, 1949, after Donald's first birthday party, a gathering of relatives at home, wherever that was, he fell asleep on the sofa; and as his mother carried him to his crib, tucked him in, and kissed his toys good night, he half woke to the rustling of her full-skirted cocktail dress of changeable taffeta, a popular fabric of the period, shimmering black green black green black green black in a sensuous poetry of flux which made a lifelong impression on him. I don't know how I know this, but in that moment he internalized a blissful, bamboozling mockery of his own intellectual rigor. When he turned five—January 10, 1953—his kindergarten teacher had him sent to a nearby college or university for I.Q. testing, a fad of the era. Little Donnie was seated in front of a board with different geometric-shaped holes in it, given a selection of geometric blocks, and told to fit each block in the correct hole. "You must be joking," he said, as with a sweep of one small hand he sent the blocks flying.

. . .

Bobby Fischer used to say things like "Crash!" and "Kaboom!" when he captured pieces. At fourteen, he won the U.S. Chess Championship—on January 7, 1958, just three days before my seventeenth birthday. He was a mysterious intimate—a peer I knew of but didn't know. A better me, out there untouchable. Hazel-eyed Bobby, however, was not the one whose passage would intersect with mine. He had been born on March 9th (or, according to one source, 12th), on a life path to Brooklyn, Cleveland, *I've Got a Secret,* Mar del Plata, Stockholm, Cuba by telex, Zagreb, Spassky, silence. Not even close.

. . .

On Janary 10, 1963, Donald's fifteenth birthday, his parents gave him a Raleigh English bike. He made his preferred sandwiches (peanut butter and marshmallow fluff), lashed his collection of 45s to the bike rack, and left home, cycling due west through Pennsylvania. Near the Maumee River in northwest Ohio, on the outskirts of Defiance, with 714 miles on the odometer, he finally realized that being a ward of the state wasn't all it was cracked up to be, and retraced his route. (I'm sure this is right about the 714, because it was also Joe Friday's badge number.)

. . .

That year, I was just out of the University of Pennsylvania and living in New York for the first time. My younger brother, Steve, was studying bad-younger-brother behavior, hanging around the city and getting in trouble. On my birthday we went to the Five Spot and heard Roland Kirk play weird instruments he'd invented and named—stritch and manzello. I don't want to name the deep trouble my brother got into around that time; it scared me, and one night I refused to let him stay in my apartment even though it was raining. I still think about this, although he forgave me and later a psychiatrist told me science couldn't say what I should have done.

. . .

Donald spent his twentieth birthday—January 10, 1968— buying a mattress for his first New York pad. He was carrying it back from Dixie Foam, balanced on his head, when he heard rolling thunder. The hard rain that had been predicted for five years began to fall, saturating the foam and turning it into a giant, burdensome, oppressive household sponge. He became a feminist.

. . .

I don't remember much about my birthdays through the nineteen-seventies, but probably they had something to do with sex.

. . .

By Donald's twenty-sixth birthday—January 10, 1974—he had wandered out to L.A. Some girlfriend called him that afternoon and asked him to meet her in fitting Room No. 7 in the lingerie department at Bullock's, in Westwood. When he pulled the curtain, he found her in there wearing nothing but a lacy black garter belt, mesh stockings, spike heels, and an apron, bending over a chafing dish and a lighted can of Sterno, making his favorite dessert, crêpes with Clementine-orange sections and Cointreau *flambés:* mother, sister, hostess, lover. . . . Bullock's pressed charges. Neither Donald nor the girlfriend served any time, but the store's inhospitality so aroused his anti-bureaucratic temperament that he stopped feeling guilty about frittering away his life at the track.

At Santa Anita, where he went most mornings, the trainers and stablehands welcomed his presence around the stalls, for he had a way with the horses. His magic was to call them by names he made up instead of the monikers laid on them by the owners. One day, after Donald had made his usual pre-race visit to the paddock, a magnificent chestnut stallion who had not lived up to his potential (neither would I if I were on the books as Can't Get Arrested), having heard for the first time what he must have felt all along was his true name, went out smoking, sprinted clear along the inside, was in full flight at midstretch, and crossed the wire with something left—winner by six lengths in the Nature vs. Nurture Futurity. This, of course, was the famed champion henceforth known unofficially as Impenetrable.

Once a few stories like that got around, Donald's services were widely sought for consultations and christenings. Among his successes over the next decade were High I.Q., the semiretired fourteen-year-old he nicknamed High Heels to inspire her stunning comeback in the 1975 Bobby Fischer Memorial Sweepstakes; 1976's Dixie Derby sensation, Marie, a big bay mare who had suffered from an aging crisis until Donald tactfully called her Philly; Changeable Taffeta (the first thoroughbred yearling he was hired to name), who in 1977 swept the Cross and Chain Handicap and the Silver

Orange Juice Cup; Booties, who won in a waltz after crashing the 1979 Dragnet Invitational; Stritch and Manzello, the siblings who took win and place for a combined purse of $850,000 in the 1981 Sterno Hospitality Classic; and the 40–1 long shot who captured the 1982 Piggie Bank Stakes, the amazing Just a Coincidence.

On Donald's thirty-fifth birthday—January 10, 1983—his secretary made a list, for thank-you notes, of the presents he got (and I believe these touched his heart more than the huge fees he commanded): white cashmere saddle blanket—Calumet Farm; gold I.D. bracelet—Mom and Dad; silk-covered hot-water bottle in black and green stripes, racing colors of Grimm Stables—Grimm brothers; silver horse-insignia roach clip—Chet (groom, Pimlico); greeting card with verse ("May life bring *EVERY* joy to bless / *Ese pequeñito sueño de FE-LICIDAD!*")—Angel Cordero.

. . .

January 10, 1988, was my forty-seventh birthday, Donald's fortieth. Some years ago he had wandered back East, to New York, and made his home here, and we'd met through my boyfriend, Jimmy, a photographer who had taken his picture. When we first found out we had the same birthday, we didn't make a big deal out of it, but as we became friends it seemed more and more significant. This year, we discussed offering ourselves for a new kind of study by those people in Minnesota who studied twins. Our hypothesis was that the many similarities in our lives formed a pattern; that discovering the pattern made us feel happy; and that our case might provide valuable data for investigating the phenomenon of friends reared apart. But we were afraid of being rebuffed as astrology cranks, or as frauds who had subjectively distorted the truth out of pure longing to have a lot in common. So, with a sweep of his hand and mine, we sent the scientific method flying, and threw a party.

DECEMBER 1987–JANUARY 1988

Long after the liner has been put in drydock
The wish still steers the rudder of its will.
They are carting away the remains of a novel
Two people worked on for years. . . .

—*Howard Moss*

Howard Moss had also been the *New Yorker*'s poetry editor, and his office was two doors away from mine. That fall, I'd been overjoyed to see him back after a leave of absence; a few days later he died. He used to come into my office to bum a cigarette just to hold, and then stand there praising a "gorgeous" poem he'd read—or he might say, "My dentist novel, *Night Cavities,* is almost finished." His book of biographical sketches, *Instant Lives,* was on my mind: "Where will it end, Liszt asked himself, preparing for another whirlwind tour of the musical centers of Europe: Lannion, Vaasa, and Bruges. Getting the piano up on the horses was not the least of his difficulties."

Howard had once told me that an important part of the work of writing is the time when you do nothing, take a walk, read for fun, go to the theater, etc. Here are some things I saw and read in the "spare time" around the writing of this story; it seems now that I'd never have tried it without them:

Burn This, Lanford Wilson's play. Standard premise (and-then-an-insane-guy-comes-in), but it used convention to carve out a big, strange space for the opposite. Joan Allen talked with extreme normalness, John Malkovich with extreme extravagance, and at the end they got together.

"Family," by Harold Brodkey (a Reflections piece in the *New Yorker*). All kinds of mental memorabilia about generations of Brodkey's relatives. Made a literary form out of coincidence and hearsay. About the past but not bound by the past, it had momentum and a final swan-dive into conviction.

Prison-Made Tuxedos, a play by George Trow. Two parallel lives. Real-life jazz saxophonist Frank Morgan was onstage, talking and playing music; in alternate scenes, an actor played a satirized version of the author. The two characters never met, but the writing and music made other encounters between them.

"Fordham Castle," in *The Marriages,* a collection of bizarrely symmetrical stories by Henry James. A man banished by his wife as an impediment to her social ambitions is traveling in Europe under a false identity, and guesses that a woman he meets is in the same boat. The "communities in their fate."

"New Year's Eve," by rock critic Lester Bangs (written in 1979, reprinted in a collection of his work, *Psychotic Reactions and Carburetor Dung,* edited by Greil Marcus). Every New Year's Eve he could remember:

> 1971: I stayed home and read the Bible. No, that's a lie. What I did was go to the drive-in with my girlfriend—all hopped up (me, that is) on vodka and her mother's thyroid pills, totally unable to concentrate on the double feature of *I Drink Your Blood* (starring Rhonda Fultz, Jadine Wong, and somebody merely billed "Bhaskar") and *I Eat Your Skin* (William Joyce, Heather Hewitt) . . . thinking all night how next morning I was gonna do like Jack Kerouac and just jump in my car eating speed with one hand while flicking the starter with the other and drive drive drive till I plashed through Blakean breakers of light on the golden prows of the Rocky Mountain Shield. Of course I didn't, woke up with a muzzy hangover instead, which is probably just as well: I coulda ended up being John Denver.

"Subconscious Mind," a dance choreographed and performed by Karole Armitage. The sound was a tape of a routine by the hipster comic Lord Buckley, the décor was a few circles and squares of color and light (including a giant square-cut "diamond" ring), and the dancer seemed pulled between the Cool and the Square.

The whole time I was writing, I denied that this story was "really about" Donald Fagen (who does have the same birthday I do). I claimed it was a cool decision to write something to get money for my half of our birthday party; that writing it about the birthday was just a handy modernist trick (make the thing about the process of making the thing, etc.); and that the "Donald" in the story was merely "a construct." *It's all right— all doctors do this.* . . . Then when I finally showed it to him and asked if I could leave his name in, I admitted it was "really about" him. It was an excuse to be romantic about our friendship.

There's nothing more fun than using your work to make a present for a friend. Much more fun than knocking things. Part of the present was giving him a collection of entirely fake memorabilia. The "You must be joking" episode with the blocks came from Nancy Cardozo and Mark Jacobson—their daughter Rae did that. The parts about me and my family, and the last section, are fact.

I'd never written so directly about myself or my family and was scared that the story was nakedly revealing and embarrassing. This isn't the detached feeling you need to fine-tune your own sentences, so I asked Harold Brodkey for help; his fiction seemed emotionally fearless, and he was always using the word "prose" around the office. He taught me to be wary of habitually writing a certain kind of sentence, with a structure he described as "Blah blah blah, *but not really.*" It's a humorist's sentence, which self-destructs—no good when you're trying to say, "Blah blah blah—fantastic though it may seem, *really.*" He also encouraged me to "hint more strongly at the idea of two common souls separated in another life, or something like that." This was the kind of suggestion that emboldens you in what you tentatively, secretly hoped to do. I'd been leafing through Joseph Campbell's *The Hero with a Thousand Faces* (looking for what he had on the Sleeping Beauty story), and had copied out these four sentences:

> Another image of indestructibility is represented in the folk idea of the spiritual "double"—an external soul not afflicted by the losses and injuries of the present body, but existing safely in some place removed.

> Sequences of events from the corners of the world will gradually draw together, and miracles of coincidence bring the inevitable to pass.

> [Sleeping Beauty] "opened her eyes, awoke, and looked at him in friendship."

> All existence . . . may at last be transmuted into the semblance of a lightly passing, recurrent, mere childhood dream of bliss and fright.

Liz Macklin, an editor at the office, got a friend of hers, Arnaldo Sepúlveda, to do the Spanish translation for the verse for Angel Cordero's birthday card. I'd expected anything in Spanish to look romantic, but some of the words looked normal, so I only used half of it. Later Liz said, "To my mind, two of the most beautiful words in Spanish are *brinde* and *alegría,* and you seemed to find them repellent—as if they looked like words for birth control." But then, she said, Arnaldo thought the verse in English had "no schmaltz whatsoever."